COMING HOME

COMING HOME

•

Nadia Shworan

AVALON BOOKS
NEW YORK

PRINTED IN THE UNITED STATES OF AMERICA
ON ACID-FREE PAPER
BY HADDON CRAFTSMEN, BLOOMSBURG, PENNSYLVANIA

To Mom and Dad,
who were the true romantics

Chapter One

Laura savored the peaceful privacy of the empty building. There were no pressures—no intruders to her thoughts.

The interruption came sharp and rude. "What on earth are you doing up there!"

Startled, Laura dropped the tack and, arms waving, teetered on her makeshift ladder before regaining her balance.

She recognized the voice before looking in his direction. His frame filled the doorway and his face scowled with annoyance. Same frame, same doorway, same scowl, same tone of disapproval—and for her, the same feeling of helplessness.

"Nothing," she said, her response automatic. She became acutely aware of her faded blue jeans, bare feet, and rather skimpy T-top, and she blushed as she self-consciously tugged the hem of her shirt down over her midriff.

When she had accepted the position, she knew that sooner or later she would have to face him again. She had even looked forward to it with a perplexing mixture of trepidation and anticipation. But what on earth was he doing here today? Miss Peabody had told her he would be out of town until the middle of next week.

By next week, the school would be well populated. Many of the teachers would be back, chatting about summer holidays, discussing plans for the year, setting goals, and preparing their courses. There would be old students—some of them just saying hello, others changing courses—and new ones, accompanied by anxious parents, would be getting enrolled and touring the school. And, there would be support staff. In addition to Miss Peabody, the secretary, and the caretaker, there would be paraprofessionals and volunteers rushing around, duplicating and collating all manner of handouts, helping teachers set up classrooms and labs, unpacking and organizing supplies, and generally adding to the feeling of being in a beehive. She would have been much better able to handle a meeting then.

Laura's stomach was a jumble of knots and her heartbeat sounded loud and erratic in her ears.

"You could have hurt yourself," he scolded. "Haven't you heard of ladders?"

She wished he'd stop nagging, but no chance. Michael Foster was on a roll.

"All you had to do was ask the caretaker," he continued. "You may have gotten a little older, Laura Hart, but you sure didn't pick up any more sense."

She wanted to leave, but she was trapped and vulnerable, as she stood on the little stack of dictionaries piled on a chair, on top of the teacher's desk in the middle of the classroom. Of course she had been foolish to climb up there, but she had planned to be careful. Even so, she felt the need to explain her situation to him.

"It was only one mobile," she said. "I wanted to see how it would look up there. I didn't think I needed a ladder for just that." Hearing herself babbling nervously, she became angry.

"You didn't think," he agreed.

Why was she allowing herself to be intimidated? What right did he have to patronize her? "Maybe not, but I was doing fine until you startled me," she shot back. "You have no right to yell at me."

She watched him stride toward her, a frown creasing his brow above those penetrating ice-blue eyes. How many times had she seen him come into this very room just that way?

"I'm not a child," she added, and then realized that just by saying it, she sounded childish.

"Then stop acting like one. Get down off that chair before you break your neck." He reached out to help her.

"I can get myself down." She pushed his hands away and threw herself off balance. One of the dictionaries slid out from under her foot and clattered to the desk below. Michael was quick. Before she could react, his hands clasped her waist and he lifted her down.

The knots in her stomach became an intricate macramé. She jerked free and stepped away from him, right into the corner of the teacher's desk. Pain shot up and down her leg as the rest of the dictionaries were sent clattering to the desktop and then crashing to the floor.

"See what I mean?" His eyes bored into hers.

It was all she could do to keep from crying out. The pain was excruciating. He had said she would hurt herself. Darn it, she wasn't going to give him the satisfaction of being right.

She had hoped things would be different between them now that she was no longer the rebellious student in his class, but it was as though the past ten years had never happened. In his presence, she regressed to being an insecure adolescent, and he continued to be the infuriating and insensitive adult that she remembered. Why couldn't she do anything right when he was around? And why couldn't he, just for once, see her as a person, not just a dumb kid? He could have said something pleasant like 'good to see you,' or 'welcome back,' or even just 'hello.'

"Yes," she snapped, "I do see what you mean." Eyes smarting, she studied the floor. She was angry with him, but even more, she was disappointed with herself for not being tougher. If she was going to work in the same building with him, she had to stop letting him affect her this way.

"You are hurt," he said. "I was too rough when I caught you. I'm sorry. It happened so fast I didn't have time to be careful."

She shook her head in response. "I'm fine," she said. "You didn't hurt me." But what she wanted to say was, 'You're hurting me now, just by being here.' She remembered a quotation in one of those self-help books her mother was always buying, "People can't hurt you unless you let them." So why was she letting him?

He studied her. "Are you sure? You don't look so fine."

She avoided eye contact. "I thought you were supposed to be out of town this week," she said.

He laughed. "Sorry to disappoint you. I decided not to go."

"I didn't mean—"

"I couldn't afford the time," he continued. "There's just too much to do before school starts."

They were on safe ground now. "You and I both!" she agreed.

He smiled, and she couldn't help but smile back. His look was gentle as he studied her. "Here, let me put that mobile up for you." He took the mobile she had been trying to hang. Their hands touched and there was an instant awareness—like touching a hot stove, or an electric current.

He cleared his throat. "Just tell me where you want it."

"I dropped the tack," Laura said. "It's around here somewhere." She examined the floor around the desk. It was a good excuse to get away from his magic. "Found it," she said. She bent down to get it.

He was beside her, reaching for it—too close. She picked up the tack and then, careful to avoid contact, quickly dropped it into his hand and stepped away from his force field.

Michael leaped up on the desk and, without the need of her improvised stepladder, reached up and positioned the ornament. "How's that?"

"Fine," she said.

He fastened it to the ceiling and looked down at her. "Is that where you want it?"

She nodded.

It was ironic seeing him up there, up on a pedestal. That was where he'd been right from the very first.

Nadia Shworan

It was back in the fall of Laura's senior year. There was a great deal of excitement when Michael Foster, one of the star players on the Canadian National Team, arrived to teach in Providence.

Basketball was a sacred tradition in the small-town high schools of southern Alberta. Every Friday night, whenever there was a home game, it seemed as though the whole town turned out to watch the teams play. The pressure was high to beat the teams from neighboring towns. It was a matter of honor. A good high school coach was worth his weight in gold, and if by chance he was even halfway capable as a teacher, then so much the better. It wasn't often that a small-town school could boast having a celebrity athlete to coach the senior boys. Getting Michael was a real coup for Mr. Walsh, the principal.

So when Michael came to teach at Providence High School, hopes ran high. With his expertise the senior boys had a shot at the regional basketball championship, and maybe even the provincial trophy.

Of course, the boys idolized him and, naturally, the girls all made fools of themselves over the handsome young teacher.

When Mr. Foster started an early-bird jogging club, one hundred and thirty-three students turned out for the seven-thirty a.m. run. When Mr. Foster said that spaghetti was good food before a game, spaghetti became the popular meal. When Mr. Foster said that t'ai chi helped him to be in touch with himself, everyone wanted to take t'ai chi. And when Mr. Foster said that poetry was good for the soul, poetry became popular. Granted, some of the boys never got past racy limericks.

Foster fever, they called it.

Laura wasn't immune to the infection. From the day he arrived, it was as though she was afflicted with some sort of virus. Her whole senior year was characterized by irritable tension and unbearable restlessness. She endured a constant flutter in her stomach, shortness of breath, and a semi permanent flush.

It had been a mixed-up sort of year. She was busy with many school activities and too many social ones. In her spare time, she sketched portraits of people and dogs and horses, and she painted idyllic scenes of pastures with rivers and trees and flowers. She loved to read, especially romances and fantasies. In secret, she wrote love poems, but whenever he was near, there was nothing she could do—nothing but display an unbelievable lack of intelligence and an even greater lack of common sense.

And now, as she looked around the classroom, she doubted that anything had changed. Here she was again, in the same room where Mr. Foster had been her teacher, and she was still reacting like the same feather-brained groupie. And there he was again, as patronizing as ever.

"So you've decided to come home," he said. He was standing beside her. If it had been anyone else, she wouldn't have even noticed, but with him, her comfort level was all out of whack.

She nodded and moved back a step. He was even taller and blonder and more muscular and his eyes were even bluer than she remembered. She smelled the musky odor of his after-shave. This was a new brand. Back then, he'd used Old Spice.

He was more than a desk length away, but somehow he was too near, using up all her oxygen. She tried to keep her breathing regular, but the more she tried, the more difficult it became.

There was a long silence. It was disconcerting the way he studied her face. Defiantly, she stared back, but by now his gaze had dropped and he was surveying her body. Again she was aware of her jeans and T-shirt, and she wished she'd worn something less revealing. She wanted to say something to break the silence, but she couldn't speak. What she needed was to get out of there. But first, she needed her shoes. She looked around for them. They were on the floor, right by his feet. There was no way she would go over there to get them.

He was smiling at her, and his eyes had become sky-blue, the kind of color that made you want to soar right into it. Oh, if he would only feel even a part of what she felt.

"You haven't changed much," he said.

Crash. The old hurt came rushing back. Of course she had changed. She'd been an adolescent beset by frizzy hair, pimples, and identity problems. Now she was a woman. Couldn't he tell? She glared at him. "You've talked to me for less than fifteen minutes. How the heck would you know whether I've changed or not?"

He grinned and shrugged. "Still feisty, I see."

"Feisty? You mean argumentative? Or is it quarrelsome?" she snapped. "You're the one who came in here and insulted me, sir."

"It's getting a little warm in here, or is it my imagination?" His grin broadened.

"You think I'm hot-tempered? I had every right to get upset!"

He held up his hands in surrender. "Take it easy . . ." he said.

But by now she was so angry she couldn't stop. "You don't know anything about me, Mr. Foster. You never did."

He was infuriatingly calm. "I didn't say hot-tempered. I was thinking more along the lines of 'spirited,' " he said. "But now that you point it out to me, I agree, hot-tempered probably describes you even better."

Laura bit her lip. He still had the same attitude. He had been tough on her when she was his student, and it looked as though he wasn't going to give her a chance even now.

"Well, you haven't changed much either," she snapped. "You're still arrogant and insensitive."

She picked up the dictionaries that had fallen to the floor and then, pointedly ignoring him, she strode to the bookcase and firmly placed the books on the shelf.

Michael watched her walk across the room, noting the changes. Her hair was longer, more auburn and not as curly, her trim little body had acquired some very nice curves, and even in bare feet, she walked with more poise than he remembered.

When she slammed the dictionaries into the bookcase, he couldn't help but grin. No, she hadn't changed much. She still had the same volatile temper that he remembered. Whether she admitted it or not, she was feisty. This year was going to be a challenge, all right. His first year as principal had just barely started and already he had alienated one of his teachers.

He occupied himself by lifting the chair off the teacher's desk and tucking it neatly in place as he waited for her to cool down. What the heck had he said to bring all that wrath upon himself? He'd been upset with her for taking such a chance of getting hurt, but she certainly couldn't blame him for being concerned. If she had fallen from that perch she would certainly have broken an arm or a leg, or maybe even worse. But what did he say to upset her? He had no idea. Maybe she was right. Maybe he was insensitive.

But arrogant? No, not arrogant. Not now, and especially not then. That was certainly not the way he would have described himself.

He had been scared stiff.

It was his first year of teaching and he had been assigned the senior English course. For a physical education major who enjoyed a good book once in a while, when he wasn't too busy or too tired, the idea of teaching Shakespeare to a class of seventeen-year-olds had been downright scary. What if the students discovered how little he actually knew? What if he lost control of the class? What if they found him boring? He had worried about being a good teacher, about having his students do well, about turning them on to learning.

And worst of all, he had been terrified of the bubbly little redhead with dark inquiring eyes. She had made him question himself more than anyone else ever had. She had studied him with that clear-eyed, no-nonsense look and asked, "Why?" and "What does this mean?" He knew that she had been well aware whenever he didn't know the answers. She had constantly defied him. Those dark fringed eyes had stared him down and dared him to stay in control.

He had been afraid of her, all right. At twenty-two, he wasn't much more than a kid himself.

Had she really thought him arrogant? How could

she have? Laura who had often made him feel like a bumbling fool? He was impatient to continue the conversation. She finally turned his way.

"Did you really find me arrogant?" he asked.

She avoided his gaze and ignored his question.

"I certainly didn't feel arrogant," he said.

She shook her head. "I'm sorry, I shouldn't have said that. I just lost my temper. Maybe I am 'feisty' after all."

He watched her bite her lip in frustration. "No, don't apologize," he said. "I'm the one who should be apologizing for upsetting you."

She didn't reply. Was it tacit agreement?

"To tell the truth, that was a tough year for me. It was my first year teaching. I tried to do a good job," he said. "If I seemed arrogant, it was probably because I was trying too hard."

"Well you didn't try very hard with me."

She knew how to draw blood. "That was quite a statement, Laura. What exactly do you mean by it?"

"Nothing."

"No, not nothing. You can't just say something like that and leave it hanging there. Please tell me what you meant. I really want to know." He waited a long, pregnant moment but she didn't reply.

"Talk to me, Laura. Play fair with me. How do you expect me to change my behavior if I don't know what I'm doing wrong?"

She shrugged. "Well," she said. "It sounds so petty when I talk about it, but it's just that you always seemed to have time for everybody else but you never had time for me. You made it very obvious that you didn't like me."

"I didn't like you? Is that what you thought?"

She shrugged. "It doesn't matter."

He took a step toward her. "But it's not true, Laura. You couldn't have been more wrong."

She took a step back. "It's not important," she said. "Thank you very much for helping me with the mobile, Mr. Foster."

"I did like you, Laura. Oh sure, there were many times when I wanted to give you a good shake and tell you to smarten up."

"That's all you ever did say to me."

"Come on, Laura, that's not exactly true. You must admit that you were a brat in my class. You made no effort to do well in your schoolwork. All you did was chat with your friends, fool around, and talk back."

"See what I mean?"

"But, in spite of that, I liked you. I could see a lot of potential. I just didn't know how to tap it."

Laura made no comment and he went on, "I was obviously right about the potential. Look at you now. You are a teacher and you have come highly recommended," he said. "And please call me Michael. I'm not your teacher anymore."

"No, now you're my boss," she said. She slipped her feet into her sandals and went to the shelf by the windows where she had left her things.

Her hair shone copper and gold in the sunlight. She slipped on her sweater and picked up her purse.

"Will you be back before school starts?" he asked.

"Probably." She took an armful of books and binders from the shelf and walked the long way around the room to get to the door. "I have a lot to prepare—outlines, units—plus, I have to set up my classroom . . ."

She was obviously avoiding him. Why? She couldn't

possibly be afraid of him, could she? He had rubbed her the wrong way. He wished he hadn't. He should have known better than to even try to communicate with her. He recalled that she used to bristle at his every comment, and somehow, his every comment to her had come out wrong. She was like a kitten, hissing and spitting for protection.

He wanted things to be different this time. He didn't want her to leave like this. "If you need any books, supplies, anything, let me know," he said, trying to prolong the conversation.

Laura gave him a curt nod. "I'll be fine, thank you. You really don't have to bother with me. I talked to Miss Peabody. She said she'll be here all week. I can get all my supplies from her." Her face had become expressionless, her voice flat.

"It's no bother. I'm going to be here every day."

"I imagine that goes with your new job," she said. "I guess I should congratulate you."

"Not unless you mean it."

She sure didn't sound congratulatory, Michael thought. She had seemed to warm up a little but now he was back in the deep freeze. What had he done to merit it? He mentally reviewed what he had said or done that might have upset her—nothing.

Laura ignored his comment. "I know I wouldn't have been your choice as a new staff member. You're probably sorry you got stuck with me."

"I'm not complaining."

"I'm a good teacher," she said. "I'll do a good job."

"I never thought otherwise."

Laura studied him for a moment. "Right!" she said, and she walked out the door.

Michael watched her walking away from him down the hall.

That was it! She was still angry over something he had done years ago. But what? He racked his brains.

As far as he knew, he hadn't done anything. He had been careful to avoid being alone with her, to sidestep too much interaction.

But he must have done something. She hadn't liked him much even then. She'd been so blatantly obvious in her disapproval. He had always felt that she was evaluating him and finding him inadequate.

She had made him feel insecure his first year as a teacher. It looked as though she would make his first year as the principal just as insecure.

Michael headed for the gymnasium. He needed to shoot some baskets. Basketball usually helped him relax.

Chapter Two

By the time Laura got to her car, she was shaking. She started the engine, stepped down hard on the gas pedal, and left the school parking lot in a cloud of dust and gravel spray. She had made a mess of it again. The quicker she got out of there, the better.

She had thought she was over him, but being here and seeing him again, all the old feelings came rushing back.

Grade twelve—she had been seventeen and wanted desperately for the young teacher to notice her. He had come into town straight out of some dream. At first, she had tried staying in the classroom after school, asking him for extra help, but that didn't seem to work. At least half the class—no, half the school— had the same idea. His classroom was always full of students, so that whenever Michael Foster got around to talking to her, she was always part of a group. No matter how well she had planned it, it never worked

15

out. She had zero time alone with him. On a couple of occasions, she outlasted the other students, but even then, she didn't get his undivided attention. On those occasions when, finally, she was the only one left and there was no one else around to grab his attention, he would look at his watch, grab his briefcase, and dash out the door.

The first time it happened, she had stayed behind to get some help interpreting one of Robert Frost's poems, "Stopping by Woods on a Snowy Evening." She had dawdled, taking her time finishing her work and putting her books away, and then she had waited for the other students to leave. When the last student said good-bye and walked out the door, Laura was alone with her hero, Michael Foster. Finally, it was her turn.

She sidled up to his desk and said, "I'm having trouble with the poetry assignment, Mr. Foster." When he looked up, she added, "Frost's poem. I'm not sure what it means when it says 'And miles to go before I sleep' twice at the end of the poem."

All of a sudden, Michael Foster was just too busy to spend another moment with her. "I'm sorry, Laura, I can't stay to help you," he said. "Read it again. I'm sure you'll figure it out yourself."

"It'll just take a minute . . ." she said.

"Don't worry about it. We'll discuss the poem in class. I've got to go." And he had dashed out the door and down the hall.

It had been pretty obvious to Laura that he had not wanted her to stay. As far as she was aware, he never took off like that when other students came to him for help.

The fact that she didn't really need any help may have had something to do with it, but Laura had not considered that possibility. She had been a good student, near the top of her class all through school, and there were many other students who needed tutoring more than she did, but knowing that didn't make her feel any better.

Even during class time, Mr. Foster seemed to spend all his time with the others. She begrudged the attention he gave them and resented the fact that he was always too busy for her.

It was the tenth of February, four days before Valentine's Day, and the class was studying Shakespeare's *Romeo and Juliet*. Laura's mind had been a million miles from schoolwork. She was drawing intricate designs on her page—vines with heart-shaped leaves, clusters of heart-grapes, and intricate heart-flowers.

Mr. Foster—Michael—was discussing the assignment.

"All right class, we viewed the film, we read some scenes aloud in class, and we discussed the Prologue and Act I. Now it's time for you to show me what you know. I've got a question sheet for you. Put all the answers in your notebooks. Make your answers thorough and complete. You shouldn't have any trouble, but I'll be around if you need help. Okay?" He surveyed his class. There were no questions.

"Okay." He handed question sheets to the students in the front row. "Please take one and hand the rest back," he said. "You can start as soon as you get the question sheet."

Bobby Berent called out, "Hey, coach." Bobby was not one to wait his turn. He was good at sports, but not so good at sitting quietly and doing schoolwork.

Even after twelve years of being a student, he was still in the habit of calling out.

Mr. Foster smiled and shook his head at Bobby's impatience. "What's the problem, Bobby? Next time, just put up your hand."

"Okay." Bobby was easygoing. "But why can't we write on the question sheet?"

"Not enough room. Put the answers in your notebooks."

Michael Foster walked up the first aisle and Laura noticed that he had something to say to each student. She pretended not to pay attention, but her eyes kept glancing in his direction and her ears were tuned in to his voice. She heard the exchange between Mr. Foster and her friend Mary.

"Okay, Mary, how does Shakespeare inform us about the feud between the Montagues and the Capulets?"

"I don't know."

"I'll give you a hint. It happens very early in the play. See if you can find it."

Mary pointed a finger at the page. "Is this it?"

Mr. Foster gave her a big smile. "Right! Now write down the answer. What part of the play is it? Who is doing the talking? What does he say?" Laura felt a twinge of jealousy. Mary was one of her best friends but she wasn't nearly as smart as Laura. How did she rate a special smile?

He moved on to the next student. "How's it going, Mike?"

"Okay."

"Any problems?"

"No."

Then the next student, and the next.

Laura continued to doodle. She sat in the farthest row, the one by the windows. By the time Michael Foster got to her desk, her vines had become a string of intricate, well-concealed M's.

Laura had loved the story of Romeo and Juliet. She found it very romantic the way they saw each other across the room and fell in love, and very sad that the lovers couldn't be together.

She sensed the teacher's presence behind her but she didn't hide her doodles. He stood looking over her shoulder.

"What are you doing, Laura?"

She looked up at him. He frowned at her. She shrugged.

"Have you done the questions?"

"No."

"Get to work. Stop wasting time."

She wanted him to stay and talk to her, so she threw out the first question that came to mind. "What am I supposed to do?"

"I've already explained it several times. Why don't you pay attention?" He picked up the question sheet from the edge of her desk and held it inches from her face. "Answer these questions," he said. He put the sheet down in front of her and pointed to the page with the doodles. "Put the answers in your notebook." He sounded exasperated.

She didn't want him to be upset with her. Laura stared at the paper but the question blurred. "I can't do it," she said.

"Now what's the matter?" he asked.

What could she tell him? That she was crying? No way. "I don't understand that old-fashioned English."

Now he really sounded exasperated. "We saw the

film. We read the play in class. We discussed it. How could you not understand it? Where was your head? In dreamland?" he asked.

She shrugged. She'd paid attention. She loved the movie. She'd played the balcony scene in her head a million times, imagining that he was her Romeo and she was Juliet. But she wasn't about to tell him that. That was her secret. Nobody would know. She printed ROMEO AND JULIET at the top of her page but she put a fancy capital M in the middle of Romeo and a capital L in the middle of Juliet. Let him figure that out if he was so smart.

"Well, if you don't know what the play is about, then read it again," he commanded.

"The play is about love," she said. "But you're so mean you wouldn't know anything about that."

He stood looking at her, not saying anything. He didn't seem to know what to do about her, and she was kind of enjoying making him mad, so she added, "What's the use of reading something that's totally weird?"

He shook his head and walked away. She watched him bend over to help one of the other students. The show was over. She got to work on the assignment.

The next day, when he saw her completed work, instead of praise, he gave her another lecture. "You see," he said, "there's nothing to it, if you only take the time to think things through."

It seemed to her that the only time he actually noticed her was when she did something wrong.

So she stopped trying to please him, and wonder of wonders, that was when she got his attention.

She submitted mediocre reports, first drafts, and incomplete assignments. And he tossed them back at her. "Rewrite. Finish. You can do better than that."

"No I can't," she retorted.

"What's wrong with you, Laura?" he asked. "You have the ability. Why don't you apply yourself?"

She gave him a wish-you-were-dead look. "What do you care what I do?"

He looked hurt, and she felt triumphant. It gave her a feeling of power to know that she could make him react. It wasn't the type of reaction she wanted from him, but at least he never got quite as mad at anyone else.

"As far as you're concerned, I'm just a stupid kid."

"That's what you want us to think. Isn't that right, Laura? You are doing everything you can to make us believe it." His eyes got icier than she had ever seen them, and his voice was acid. "There's nothing wrong with your ability, Laura—nothing that a good spanking wouldn't cure. Get serious about your work! Keep this up, and you won't amount to a hill of beans," he lashed back at her. With that, he went to the next student.

Laura muttered, "You're not fair!" and stuck out her tongue at him behind his back.

Now she wondered at the perversity of fate. When she'd left Providence, she had intended to never come back. She had planned to study, travel, live in a city, have adventures, date interesting men, and most of all, amount to something so she could prove Michael wrong.

In her imagination, she had visualized herself as being famous, with Michael reading about her successes or seeing her interviewed on television. "That's Laura," he would say. "She's really turned out to be a remarkable person. I misjudged her." He would ask her to come back to Providence and marry him, but she wouldn't. She would have outgrown the little town and her childish crush.

Thinking back, now with a teacher's perspective, Laura felt more than a little guilty for the way she had misbehaved in his class. It must have been hard for him, a first-year teacher, to cope with all that adulation, but he hadn't allowed the hero worship to go to his head. Somehow, he had seemed almost unaware of it. Maybe he was so used to it that it didn't affect him.

Ironically, once she got away from Providence and the farm, the things she enjoyed doing the most were the things she had done back home. She loved to read and paint landscapes and, especially, to drive past the city limits to where the farms and ranches began. As for city men, they had been no different from the fellows she had grown up with. There had been dates, but no fireworks. No one had ever made her giddy, not like Michael had. And as for amounting to something, she was beginning to realize that it all depended on one's definition of success.

Success equaled happiness, which equaled Michael. But she and Michael had been from two different sides of the teacher's desk. They might as well have been from two different planets. No matter how hard she had tried, he had treated her as just a kid. Now he was her principal, and nothing had changed between them. Once the teacher's desk had blocked her from his view. Now his office door would be the barrier.

As she approached the edge of town, she noticed the service station on the corner, Sweeny's Garage. She looked down at her gas gauge. She was down below a quarter tank. May as well stop for a fill-up. She pulled up to a pump and dug into her purse for her credit card.

"It's Laura Hart, isn't it?" The man took off his cap and wiped his forehead with his sleeve. "My, but you've turned out fine. City life must be agreeing with you."

"Hello, Mr. Sweeny." Laura smiled at the station attendant. "You don't look so bad yourself." He had been the owner-operator ever since she could remember.

He grinned back. "Can't complain. Got my health," he said. He removed the gas cap, inserted the nozzle into her gas tank, and asked, "Want me to fill'er up?"

She nodded.

He started the pump. "Saw your dad a while ago. Said you were coming home to help out, with your mom sick and all. How is she doing, anyway?"

"She's doing fine, I think. It's hard to tell with Mom. She's not one to let on when she's not feeling well."

"Probably doesn't want you to worry," he said, cleaning her windshield. "Haven't seen your brother in years. I told your dad he should retire—move to Arizona and let your brother take over the farm."

Laura shook her head. "I don't think my brother is interested in farming, Mr. Sweeny."

"He had some sort of big, important job in the States, last I heard. Is he still there? What is he doing?"

"Yes, he's still in California, working with computers," she said. "He doesn't get back very often, but he is planning to come home for Christmas."

"What about your sister? How's she doing?"

"She's fine."

He finished with the windshield and came back to the pump. "Your dad says she's in Calgary but she don't come down much."

"Her husband has problems with allergies so they don't come to the farm very often."

"You don't say. What all is he allergic to?"

"Oh, dogs, horses, cats, dust, pollen, and I don't know what else . . ."

"All the things there's plenty of out on a farm," he said. "I guess that just leaves you to take over. You need to get yourself a good man and settle down on the homestead. Give your folks a chance to take it easy."

Laura laughed. "All the good men are already taken."

"There's still a few of them around. The Berent boy comes by here every so often. I hear say he's been waiting for you."

"You mustn't believe everything you hear."

"Maybe not," he said. "But I still say young Berent's a fine young man, and a good farmer to boot. A girl can't do much better'n that."

Laura hurried to change the subject. "What about your family? How's Mrs. Sweeny?"

"She's still fat and sassy, happy as could be. She's got the grandkids down for a couple of weeks and she's been cooking up a storm. Marlene's kids." He shook his head. "Too bad they don't live close by. Then we could see them more often."

"Where do Marlene and her family live now?"

"Lethbridge, same as half the kids from here. It's a shame. All the young people are running off to the city. Just us old folks left here. Who's going to be left to do the farming?"

"The town seems to be doing all right," Laura said. "The school seems to be holding its own."

The pump stopped. Mr. Sweeny squeezed another twenty cents' worth into her tank, returned the nozzle to the pump, and put the gas cap back on before replying.

"Doesn't make sense, does it?" He looked at the display on the gas pump. "That'll be eighteen bucks."

Laura handed him her credit card and waited for him to return. He had a point there. Both her brother and sister had left the farm with no intention of returning. So it had been left up to her to volunteer to come home.

"They say you're a teacher now."

Laura smiled. "I'll be teaching at the high school."

"Good for you, girl! You heard Walsh got to be the superintendent and young Foster is the principal now." He handed her the clipboard.

Laura nodded.

"Now there's a nice young man for some girl."

She took her credit card, signed the form, and handed it back to him. "Thanks, Mr. Sweeny," she said. She started the engine. "Say hello to the family for me."

He gave her a broad grin. "Will do," he said. "And good luck in your new job!"

She waved and drove off. She might need luck at that.

Getting a teaching job in her home town had been surprisingly easy. She had telephoned Mr. Walsh, her high school principal, to see if there was an opening. There was. She applied, and within a couple of days,

Mr. Walsh called her back to tell her that she could begin working there in the fall, teaching high school English.

She had wondered about Michael. Was he leaving? Had he already left? She had wanted to ask Mr. Walsh, but she didn't have the nerve. She didn't want him to put two and two together and come up with some ridiculous number.

It was about a week later that her mother had telephoned and passed on the news that Mr. Walsh was going to be the new superintendent of schools for the region.

"One of the teachers is taking over as principal," her mother said. "I think it's that awful man who always picked on you. You know who I mean."

"Nobody picked on me, Mom."

"Sure, remember that basketball coach. You were in his class. You said he never had time to teach you anything."

Laura felt her throat tighten. "Who?"

Her mother was obviously enjoying passing on the town's latest gossip. "I remember Bobby liked him. He and you got into such an argument over that teacher. You said that no wonder Bobby liked him, he was high scorer on the basketball team, and the only people he helped were the boys on his team."

Laura's heart skipped a beat. "Michael Foster?"

"That's him—the only teacher that ever phoned to complain about you. You don't have to work there, you know."

Laura regained her composure. "Are you saying he's the principal now?"

"That's what I hear," her mother confirmed. "I feel sorry for you having to work with him."

"Don't worry, Mom. I'll be all right."

And she meant it—even though she still ached when she remembered his rejection of her, still had trouble understanding why he hadn't liked her. And she still felt embarrassed by the memory of her foolish crush.

Chapter Three

"Look out, Shep, you big old mutt!" Laura said to the big orange dog prancing excitedly all around her. Shep was old, arthritic, and hard of hearing, but since Laura had returned home, he acted like a pup and was constantly underfoot. She bent down to scratch behind his ears, and the dog groaned with contentment. "Come on, let's go home."

She picked up the books from the passenger seat of her car, shut the car door, and walked to the house. Shep stayed so close beside her that his tail slapped her leg, and he got in her way as she walked.

She pulled open the screen door and called out just as she always had, "Hi, Mom, I'm home."

There was no reply. Her mother must be sleeping. Laura cushioned the screen to keep it from slamming and then slipped off her shoes and padded barefoot into the kitchen. She could hear the abrasive sounds of talk show voices coming from the living room, so she deposited her books on the kitchen counter and went to investigate.

Sure enough, she found her mother dozing in the big recliner, oblivious to the heated discussion on the television screen. Laura studied her mother's thin pale face, noting the dark hollows under her eyes. Did they seem darker?

Mrs. Hart opened her eyes and smiled at her daughter.

"Hi, Mom." Laura kissed her mother's forehead. "How was your morning?"

Her mother pushed the mute button on the remote control. "Hi, dear. I didn't hear you come in."

"The TV was pretty loud and I was pretty quiet. I hope you haven't tired yourself out," Laura scolded.

"Don't worry so much. I haven't done a thing but watch television all morning," Mrs. Hart said. "And you, dear? How was school? Did you manage to get yourself organized?"

Laura shook her head. "There's still so much to do. It's a new job for me and a new grade." She returned to the kitchen and looked in the refrigerator. "I'm starved. Did you and Dad have lunch yet?"

"Dad ate some of that stew you made," Mrs. Hart said. "There's still some left in the pot. Why don't you have some?"

Laura filled a bowl with the thick aromatic mixture of meat and vegetables. "How was it?" she asked, bringing her food into the living room.

"Your father had seconds."

Laura put a place-mat on the coffee table and set the bowl down on top of it. "And what about you, Mom? How much did you eat?"

"Please stop fussing over me. I'm doing just fine."

As far back as Laura could remember, her mother had always been a dynamo of energy—never too sick to cook and clean and look after her husband and children. When the stomachaches had started, she had called them indigestion. "When you get older, you have to expect a few discomforts," she had said.

It was when they had all gotten together at Easter that they had finally convinced her to see a doctor. It had all happened so quickly—the tests, the ultrasounds, the x-rays. Her mother had stomach cancer.

After surgery she had to have more tests, more x-rays, and more prayers that the cancer would not recur. But there wasn't much hope for recovery. Life wasn't always fair.

Laura's father was a farmer. He loved the farm, but the way things were going, he would have to sell. It would be sad to see the old home place go to strangers, but Dad was getting older and Mom might not make it. Laura couldn't imagine her father living out here alone, or anywhere else, without her mother.

Her mother interrupted her thoughts. "How did you enjoy going back to the school?"

"Fine, Mom." She took a mouthful of stew. It did taste good. "This stew turned out all right," she said. "I'd better make some more to put in the freezer. That way you and Dad can have stew for lunch once in a while." Maybe she should consider preparing a series of freezer lunches for her parents. She'd better get at it before school started.

"It was a funny feeling being back at the school," Laura said.

"Funny? How do you mean?"

"At first, I felt like an intruder, like a student with the teacher's keys. There were just the exit lights above the doors and whatever light came through the transoms above the classroom doors, so the halls were quite dark. It was eerie and almost too quiet. I'd never been there when it was so quiet. I could hear my running shoes whisper, and I could see my reflection in the freshly polished floor."

"Your shoes whispered, did they?" her mother teased. "It sounds to me like you've had your nose in one too many of those poetry books you always carried around with you."

"There's nothing wrong with poetry, Mom."

"No, I guess not. Is Lila Peabody still there?"

Laura grinned. "She was there in the morning. You wouldn't believe it, Mom but she's still the same. Her desk is still in the same spot, and she clacks away on the same old typewriter. There's still a basket of dried flowers on the intercom, and I wouldn't be surprised if they were the same old flowers. She treated me like one of the kids—told me not to lose my keys."

"I'm sure that to her, you still *are* one of the kids. She's been in that school a long time. She was there way before Mr. Walsh's time."

"How could she stay cooped up in the same old school all her life? I sure couldn't."

"That's what you think because you're still so young. Young people are restless," Mrs. Hart said. "Wait and see—when you get older, you'll find that there's comfort and security in the old familiar places."

"I'm not that young, and I'm not that restless, Mom. How old do you think Miss Peabody is?"

Mrs. Hart laughed. "She's not as old as all that. You young people see us all as having one foot in the grave."

Laura sobered. She felt a lump grow in her throat. How could her mother joke about death?

"And as far as staying in one place all her life, when you're in the right place, it can be real nice," her mother said. "You're a dreamer, Laura. You think life is just like the fairy tales. One of these days you're going to find out that real life with a good man can be much more satisfying than a fairy tale."

"Haven't you ever wanted to be somewhere else?"

"I suppose I was like everybody else when I was young. Sure, I wanted to see the world, but then I married your dad and then you kids came along. That was all the world I ever needed."

"Not me," Laura said. "I would feel caged." She picked up her bowl and spoon, took them into the kitchen, washed them, and put them away. Then she put the leftover stew in the fridge, cleaned off the counter, and returned to the living room.

Her mother was stuck on the same topic. "You won't feel caged," she continued. "Wait until you marry and start your own family. You'll see."

Laura wiped the coffee table. Maybe her mother was right. What she needed was the right man. She thought of Michael. She and Michael in a little house in the middle of nowhere. She turned to her mother. "I'm going to be doing some school work at the kitchen table. If you need anything, Mom, just call."

"Don't worry about me, dear. I'll be fine." Mrs. Hart dismissed her with a wave of her hand.

Laura spread out her books, and soon she could hear the television again: soap opera characters professing their undying love. Laura got to work.

She looked at the course of study. What concepts were the students supposed to learn this year? What skills should they have by the end of the year? How was she going to do it?

Later her mother came into the kitchen, filled the kettle, and plugged it in. "Would you like some tea?"

"A cup of tea would be great, but sit down. Let me fix it."

"No, no, I can make the tea. It's good for me to do something once in a while." She set out two cups, put a tea bag in the teapot, and sat in the chair across from her daughter while waiting for the water to boil. "Speaking of fine young men . . ."

Laura laughed. It was just like her mother to jump into a new topic like that. "Who was speaking of fine young men, Mom?"

"Bobby Berent came over this morning. He asked about you."

"Bobby?" Laura said. "How is he? It's been a long time since I've seen him."

The kettle whistled its readiness, and Mrs. Hart got up and poured boiling water into the teapot. "Oh, he's fine, dear. As a matter of fact, he's out there right now, helping your dad." She indicated the line of machinery at the far end of the yard.

Laura waited to hear where the conversation was leading. Her mother obviously had something up her sleeve.

"I invited him for supper. You don't mind, do you?"

Laura smiled at her mother. "No, I don't mind. It'll be good to see him."

"That's what I told your dad, that it was time to get you two together again." She gave Laura a self-satisfied grin.

"No, Mom, please don't get any ideas about Bobby and me."

"Why not? You've always liked him."

"Because." Laura put her pen down. "I'd better think about getting supper started. I was so wrapped up in these books that I forgot all about food."

Mrs. Hart smiled. "I took a roast out of the freezer."

"You're not supposed to be bending or lifting or running up and down the stairs," Laura scolded. Her mother needed all the rest she could get if her body was to fight the disease.

"You worry too much." Mrs. Hart took another sip of her tea. "I think apple pie would be nice for dessert, don't you? I could sit here and peel the apples while you make the crust."

"Apple pie sounds wonderful, but I'll peel the apples, Mom. You just sit there and make sure I do it right."

"Oh, don't make such a fuss. I need to feel useful, and peeling apples isn't hard work."

"All right," Laura conceded. "Is there any ice cream in the freezer? We may as well go all the way and have hot apple pie à la mode." Laura looked at her mother.

Mrs. Hart shook her head. "There is none left. Your father and I don't eat much ice cream, so I don't usually keep it."

"No problem," Laura said. "I'll get the meal going, then I'll zip to town for a bucket of ice cream."

"Bobby would like that. You know he's been working his father's farm practically by himself this past year?" her mother said. "He plans to take it over when his father retires."

"That's what he always wanted to do." Laura took the roasting pan out of the cupboard and turned on the oven. "Where did you put the roast?"

"Defrosting in the microwave," her mother said. "He's still single and still waiting for you."

Laura hadn't expected her mother to start matchmaking this soon. "Don't even think about it, Mom," Laura said. "I'm not interested in settling down with Bobby Berent, or anybody else for that matter."

Laura drove to town and parked her car in front of Providence Foods, the biggest and the only grocery store for miles around. It was a family run store which had begun as a small shop but had expanded through the years to take over the stores on either side. Now it took pride in selling almost anything that anyone could possibly want, from fishing licenses and canned rattlesnake to cut flowers and beaded purses.

Through the large window, Laura saw Michael at one of the two checkout counters. Strange—it seemed that every time she turned around she ran into him. Well, twice so far today. Providence was a small town.

She looked in the rear-view mirror, checking her reflection. She looked anything but glamorous. She'd been driving with the window open and her hair was awry, plus she hadn't bothered to put on any makeup. It was too late to comb her hair or put on lipstick. Michael might catch her at it, and she certainly didn't want him to think she was primping just for him.

He looked out the window and grinned right at her. He'd seen her. There was nothing she could do but acknowledge him.

He came out of the store and strode toward her car. He rested a hand on the open window and held his bag of groceries in his other arm.

"Hi, Laura. Nice car." He leaned in close and smiled. It was the eyes and the teeth that dazzled her— and the hair and the body and . . .

She felt weak. "Hi, and thank you." She smiled back at him.

There was no way to leave now. She couldn't open the door, and she'd look foolish driving away. Laura felt trapped.

Being trapped felt good. She searched for something to say. There were a couple of paperback books sticking out the top of his shopping bag. He obviously liked to read.

"I see you bought some books."

He nodded. "A couple of best sellers. *The Sicilian* by Puzo and Stephen King's newest one, *The Talisman*."

Laura grimaced. "Great bedtime reading."

Michael laughed. "King's books, especially, provide interesting dreams. But what about you? What sort of books do you read? The last time I saw you, you had just discovered Tolkien. Do you still read fantasy?"

Laura was amazed. He had noticed what she was reading—he had noticed and he had remembered. "I'm surprised you remember. Yeah, I still like fantasy, but I've gotten to like other books too. Lately, I've been reading spy thrillers."

"Spy thrillers? I've pulled together quite a collection of those. You're welcome to borrow any of my books."

"Thanks, but I have enough to keep me busy. I doubt I'll have much time to read this year."

"The offer's open. You can come and borrow books anytime . . ." he said.

Laura felt herself blush. Go to his place, look at his books? He had to be kidding.

Michael continued as though he hadn't noticed the

redness of her cheeks, "I can bring the books to school if there's anything special you want to read."

Laura had trouble thinking of a response. "Maybe. Thanks for the offer."

"I see your old boyfriend Bobby Berent around once in a while," he said.

She made no comment.

"Are you still seeing him? I mean, will you be seeing him soon?" He sounded offhand, like it didn't matter to him. Well, why should it matter to him?

"Tonight," she replied. "Why do you ask?"

Michael straightened up and let go of her car. "I might need some help with the coaching this year. Would you mind telling him for me? He might be interested."

"Okay, I'll tell him," she said. "Excuse me, I've got to get some groceries. I'm in a hurry." She opened her car door and he backed away.

"Sure," he said.

Michael hadn't planned on getting Bobby to help coach, but when Laura asked him why he wanted to know if she was seeing Bobby, he couldn't tell the truth—that he just wanted to know, that he was hoping . . . So he had said the first thing that had come to mind. Surprisingly, it was a great idea.

Bobby Berent had been the best forward on the squad. He was quick and he was accurate. He could spot a hole in the defense and be in for a lay-up just like that. When it came to sports, Bobby was a tiger. At any other time, he was one of the gentlest, most easygoing boys in the school.

It was the South Alberta Championship game. The Providence Patriots were playing the Lethbridge Central Colts. The neutral court was the Fort MacLeod High School gymnasium.

The team traveled by school bus—boys boisterous in the back and cheerleaders chanting loudly at the front while the girls' chaperone, Aggie Hanes, egged them on. Michael drove.

"We're the Patriots and we know it, clap your hands. We're the Patriots and we know it, clap your hands. We're the Patriots and we know it, and we're not afraid to show it, we're the Patriots and we know it, clap your hands."

He looked in the rear-view mirror. This could be a great night for them. They were a good team. Al and John were tough on defense, and Jake, Bobby, and Frank were dynamite on offense. On top of that, the team had depth. The second string was young but they knew how play. They had a good chance of winning. If they didn't choke up, the Patriots might just come home with the trophy.

"We're the Patriots and we know it, stomp your feet . . ." the girls continued with the second verse. The boys joined in the foot-stomping.

Michael smiled to himself. Their spirits were good. Lethbridge Central with its eighteen hundred students might be over ten times bigger, but the Providence team wasn't worrying about it, at least not yet.

"Two, four, six, eight, who do we appreciate? Patriots, Patriots, rah, rah, Patriots!"

"I hope the girls have some voices left for the game," he said to Aggie.

"Don't worry," she replied. "They'll even have voices enough to cheer us home after the game."

The game was everything it was supposed to be—tight and fast and high scoring. The Patriots came out like locusts and immediately scored. First a lay-up by Bobby and then a three-pointer from John. Five to zero. The girls went wild. The Providence fans went crazy. Then the Lethbridge Central team scored, then Providence. Back and forth and back and forth.

By half time, the score was 54–48 for the Central Colts. Nothing to worry about if the boys didn't get discouraged.

Michael gathered his team around him and gave them a pep talk. Then he went on to discuss strategy. The other team was bigger but they didn't have the speed. Whenever the Patriots moved the ball fast, the Colts got flustered and left openings.

"We've got to make quick passes. Move that ball around and as soon as there's an opening, shoot." Then Michael went on to give specific suggestions to each of the players, and he finally concluded, "You know your own strengths. Play to your strengths. Do what you do best, the best way you can, and we'll take them." He looked around at the intense young faces. "We can take them," he repeated.

The game resumed, and the Patriots played with renewed vigor. John shot from the outside corner—54–51. Then the Colts took it back—56–51. Bobby with a lay-up—56–53.

"Go, Patriots go! Go, Patriots go!"

Then Frank put one in—56–56.

The crowd went wild. When the cheerleaders screamed out, "We're the Patriots and we know it, clap your hands," the clapping came from all over the gym, not just the Providence section of the bleachers.

Another lay-up from Bobby. 56–58, Patriots.

"Bobby, Bobby, he's our man, if he can't do it, Frankie can. Frankie, Frankie, he's our man, if he can't do it, Jake can . . ." the girls chanted. The game continued, each team inching past the other until the end. The score was 88–89 for the Patriots with less than a minute to go and the Colts bringing the ball up. It was tense—too tense—and Al fouled their player.

Colts shot twice, made one and missed one. 89–89. Now there was silence as the game resumed.

Suddenly, with seconds to go, Bobby had the ball. He broke away and the crowd started to cheer. He flew up the court and slammed it into the basket. 89–91.

The buzzer went. The game was over. The Patriots had won. Everyone went wild. There was jumping and screaming.

Laura had grabbed Michael and given him a big hug. "Way to go, coach!" she had shouted in his ear. Michael smiled at the memory. That was one of the few times that Laura had been pleasant to him. And then his ecstatic team descended on him.

On the way home in the bus, the boys and girls mixed.

Bobby and Laura sat together in one of the front seats. Bobby had his arm around her and she had her head on Bobby's shoulder, but every time Michael had looked in his rear-view mirror, her eyes had been on him.

Chapter Four

Laura set her knife and fork on the edge of her plate and watched Bobby sop up the gravy with a piece of bread.

"That was real good," he said. He put the bread in his mouth and, with a smile of satisfaction, picked up his paper napkin and wiped his mouth.

Laura noticed his big, callused hands with their work-stained knuckles. How many times had she counted on those hands to get her out of scrapes? They had been callused even then.

In the early grades, when her temper got her into trouble, Bobby had always sided with her. He had been so tough and so earnest that soon his reputation was all the protection she ever needed. No one picked a fight with Bobby, and everyone knew that she and Bobby were inseparable.

They had been twelve or thirteen when they shared cigarettes and even the occasional stolen bottle of beer out behind the barn. By the time she was fifteen, they had experimented with kissing.

"Wait till you see what we've got for dessert," she told him as she began clearing the table. "Something you used to like."

"Is it sauerkraut?" he joked.

"Close." She gave Bobby a big smile. "It's apple pie"—she paused for effect—"à la mode."

Bobby grinned. "All right!"

Laura's mother followed her into the kitchen and got the tea while Laura served the pie.

"Thanks for the meal, Mrs. Hart," Bobby said when he finished his pie. "It was great as usual."

Laura's mother beamed. She had always been very fond of Bobby. There had never been any secret about that. "Don't thank me, thank Laura. She's turned into a wonderful cook, hasn't she?"

"Mom!" Laura cautioned. "Stop building me up."

"Don't be modest, dear. Dad and I were just saying what a great homemaker you'd become."

Embarrassed by her mother's blatant attempt at impressing Bobby, Laura looked pleadingly at her father, but he was studiously inspecting the butter dish. Only the mischievous twitch at the corner of his mouth suggested that he was enjoying the situation.

Laura was not. She got up from the table, went to the kitchen, and filled the sink with hot water. Why was it that her mother felt it necessary to trap Bobby into marrying her? Bobby had been her best friend as well as her so-called boyfriend. She treasured the friendship, but as for the rest—it was impossible. He had to be discouraged from getting any ideas.

Laura squirted dishwashing detergent into the sink and started putting the dishes into the soapy water.

This is what they all wanted for her. If her mother had her way, she would be happily washing dishes for Bobby the rest of her life.

That wasn't what she wanted. It had been hard enough to convince Bobby to give up on her when she had left home to attend the university. Laura hoped that he didn't think she had come home to be with him.

"It don't surprise me that Laura's a good cook," she heard him say. "Not much she can't do. Never was."

"You're after another piece of pie, aren't you, Bobby?" she called out from the kitchen.

"I wouldn't turn it down."

There was almost half a pie left. She brought it into the dining room and set it on the table. "How about you, Dad? Can I cut you another piece?"

Her father shook his head and patted his stomach. "Not me. I'm about ready to burst."

Laura's mother patted her husband's hand. "If there's any left, you can have it for lunch tomorrow."

Laura smiled. Her mother was always looking after her father. Even now that she was so sick, she never stopped worrying about her husband's welfare. And Laura's father treated his wife in much the same way.

He was a good man, hard-working and peace-loving. He didn't usually have much to say. Her mother did most of the talking for both of them. He didn't seem to mind. As a matter of fact, he seemed to enjoy listening to her. He never said much, but when he did, they listened. They knew they could always count on him.

In many ways, Bobby was a lot like him—very firmly rooted in the earth and very much part of it: natural, honest, dependable. In looking from one to the other, she could see why her mother was so set on marrying her off to Bobby. In thirty years' time, Bobby would be just like her father.

Laura couldn't imagine herself becoming like her mother.

She cut Bobby an extra large wedge of pie. "Ice cream?" she asked, topping the pie with a big scoop of vanilla ice cream before he could respond. As far back as she could remember, Bobby always had a sweet tooth for ice cream.

Her father leaned back in his chair and waited for the young man to finish his dessert. "We did a good day's work today."

Bobby nodded. "Still a lot to do. Your combine needs overhauling. Want me to come over tomorrow and do it?"

"Isn't it nice of Bobby to come and help you, dear?" Laura's mother cooed.

"He can't always be helping me," Mr. Hart said. He turned to Bobby. "I appreciate the offer, but you've got enough to do bringing in your own crop."

"It's a little slow this year." Bobby scooped a healthy bite of pie and ice cream onto his fork. "It can wait a week or two, but from the looks of your fields, you're going to be needing to harvest real soon."

Laura's father looked up at her and smiled a message that said he approved of Bobby.

She smiled back, pretending to misunderstand the message. "Thanks, Dad, I'm glad you liked the meal," she said as she cleared his plate.

Her father turned back to Bobby. "I was thinking of cutting some barley tomorrow, now that the swather's all fixed. That field over by your place looks about ready."

Bobby nodded. "It'll be a good crop. You go ahead and swath. I can fix up the combine. I got nothing to do." He put the last mouthful of pie into his mouth.

"No need for you to do it," Laura's father said. "I'll have plenty of time to get at the combine once the swathing's done." He turned to his wife. "Have we got any toothpicks?"

Laura's mother started to get up.

"No, Mom. You just sit there. I'll get them," Laura said. "Just tell me where you keep them."

"Thanks, dear," her mother said. "They're on the top shelf in the spice cupboard."

"You can take my plate if you want. I'm done with it." Bobby handed her his plate.

Laura took it to the kitchen and soon came back with the box of toothpicks. "Here you are, Dad. Are you having problems with your teeth?"

"No, they're still okay. Better'n having dentures."

"Speaking of teeth," Bobby said, "I noticed a couple of teeth missing on the pickup. I should replace them for you, and grease the combine."

Laura's father shook his head, but Bobby insisted, "It won't take long. Maybe Laura can give me a hand, if she still knows how to work a wrench."

"I don't know," her father teased. "I think she's been in the city too long. Have a look at those fingernails."

"I can still work a wrench, and you two needn't worry about my nails."

"All right then," he said. "Tomorrow afternoon I'm coming over and we'll do it. Have your work clothes on."

"Okay," she told him. She handed him a dishtowel. "Do you still remember how to use one of these?"

"Laura," her mother reproached. "Let the men sit in the front room and talk. I'll help you with the dishes."

"No, ma'am," Bobby said, getting up from the table. "I'm good with dishes. You sit. Laura will wash and I'll dry."

When they were alone in the kitchen, Bobby asked, "How long are you planning to stay?"

"You mean Mom and Dad didn't tell you?"

He shook his head.

"I don't believe it. They're always telling everything to everybody. I'll be here all winter. I got a job teaching at the high school."

Bobby grinned like a Cheshire cat. "Great. Does that mean you'll be living at home?"

Laura nodded. "Yeah, I'm here to help out. You know my mom's been sick." She ran the dishrag over a plate, dipped the plate in the rinse water, and set it on the drying rack.

"Yeah, I know." Bobby picked it up and dried it. "Your mom seems to be doing okay today."

"We're hoping," she said. "She wants to get well, and she might just make it happen." She swished the dishrag around in the soapy water. "But Mom is always so cheerful, it's hard to know just how she's doing."

They finished the dishes in comfortable silence. Laura wiped the counters and drained the water out of the sink. Then she took the dishtowel from Bobby and hung it to dry on the oven door. "When was the last time you were in this kitchen, Bobby?"

"You mean before today? Just a couple of weeks ago."

Laura was surprised. "You're kidding. Are you here often?"

"We're neighbors," he said. "Of course I come over once in a while. You're the one who's been a stranger." His voice became soft. "We all hope you've come home to stay."

"I'm here because Mom needs me, but I can't stay, Bobby."

"Why not? You always loved the farm. You always said you'd never leave—up till that last year of high school. After that, there was no way anyone could talk you into staying."

He was right. Until then, her life had been simple. Everything had been decided. She was going to graduate, and then she was going to settle down with Bobby. But then it got complicated.

"You really changed that last year," he said. "I never could figure out what happened to you."

"I guess I grew up, Bobby. I discovered that there were other things I needed in my life."

"Like what?" Bobby's look was earnest. "It was my fault you left, wasn't it? I wanted you so bad that I drove you away."

"No, it wasn't you at all." Laura felt sorry for Bobby. The last thing in the world she ever wanted was to hurt him. "I just got restless. Suddenly, the farm, the town, all of it seemed to hem me in."

"Maybe after this year you'll change your mind."

Laura shrugged. "I don't think so. Don't expect me to go back to being the Laura you grew up with. You'll just be wasting your time."

"Let's just find out." Bobby's face broke into the familiar boyish grin, "Tell you what, how about we drive into town and take in a movie?"

Laura laughed. "Now?" She looked at the clock on the wall—eight o'clock. "It's too late."

"Well then, tomorrow?"

She shook her head. "I can't."

"Okay then, the next night. What do you say?"

"Oh, why not," she said. "Make it Wednesday. I should be ready for a break by then."

Bobby left, whistling a tune.

Laura hoped she wouldn't end up hurting him again.

She remembered graduation night. She had worn a strapless dress of white organza with a skirt like a cloud. Her hair had been styled so that the usually unruly mane was a mass of curls framing her face, and her makeup had been applied with care.

Her jewelry had consisted of drop earrings, which pointed toward her bare shoulders, and a pendant. She felt feminine and beautiful. Her father said she looked like an angel, but when Bobby had come to pick her up, his expression said it all. She was aware of the mixed images she was sending, and she loved it.

Bobby had looked pretty sharp himself in his black tuxedo. He brought her a wrist corsage of white sweetheart roses. It was a good idea, since there was nowhere to pin a corsage on her dress. Her mother must have suggested it to him.

"My, my, don't you two look wonderful tonight," her mother said. "Come on in, Bobby. We have to get a few pictures of you two. Laura's father's getting the camera."

Her father entered the room. "Hi, Bobby. You're looking pretty spiffy in that monkey suit," he said.

"Hello, Mr. Hart." Bobby held out his hand. "You don't look so bad yourself."

Her father shook hands with Bobby. "Don't get many chances to wear a suit—just weddings and graduations. From the look of you two, it's hard to tell what's the occasion this time."

"They both sound fine to me," said Bobby.

"Not to me," said Laura. "Come on, Bobby, let's go."

"Don't be in such a hurry," her father said. "Let's get you two up against that wall and snap a few pictures."

When they left, Laura's mother and father walked them to the door. "Have a good time, you two," her mother called out.

"You take good care of my girl," her father added.

"Don't worry, sir, I'll take real good care of my girl," Bobby replied, stressing the "my."

She didn't say anything. She wanted to, but she was too excited about the evening to bother setting them straight.

It was a great evening. The school gym was decorated with streamers, balloons, and crepe paper flowers. There were cut flowers on all the tables.

The graduating class consisted of thirty-two students, all wearing caps and gowns as they marched the length of the gym and went to sit on the stage. Mr. Walsh made a speech about what a wonderful class they had been and what a lot of opportunities awaited them. Then the names were called out, and Mr. Walsh handed each of them a graduation certificate. After that, they stood on the stage for a group picture and marched back out to remove the black robes.

More marching music as they returned to the gymnasium and went to sit at their tables for dinner. The meal was a roast beef dinner put on by the Ladies' Auxiliary. Then came the speeches they had all been waiting for.

Frank gave the class history. Most of them had been together since kindergarten so they had a lot of common history.

Then George gave the class prophecy, and each of the students was targeted with his crazy humor. Henry would join the space rangers and become a hermit on a distant asteroid. Frank would become a rock star— his wiggle would make him even more famous than Elvis. Laura and Bobby would get married, have a big farm, a dozen children, and win the Master Farm Family award in the year 2000.

Laura gave the valedictory address in which she thanked the parents, teachers, and classmates for their contributions to shaping the graduates into adults whose dreams and hopes and futures would make a difference.

Tables were cleared, the band arrived, and the dance began.

For the first song, the graduates were paired up. She danced with Bobby. The next one, she danced with her father. After that everyone took turns dancing with everyone else.

Michael danced with each of the girls in turn. Laura kept waiting for him to come for her, but each time, he selected one of the others instead. Finally, she was the only one he hadn't danced with. It was her turn, and she saw him coming in her direction.

At that point, Bobby came up and asked her, "Wanna dance?" His timing could not have been worse.

"Not right now, Bobby," she said. "I'm just going to sit here a while."

"Okay." Bobby sat beside her.

Mr. Foster came toward her and she could hardly

breathe. But then he just smiled and walked right on by to dance with Miss Hayle, the Home Economics teacher. Laura gritted her teeth. Why not with me? she thought. Maybe she had been mouthy in his class, but he should still dance with her if he danced with all the others. Laura got up and walked out of the gym and into the washroom. She studied herself in the mirror and practiced glaring, looking haughty, looking uninterested. If he did ask her, she'd turn him down. See how he would feel getting rejected. Then she combed her hair, touched up her lipstick, and went back into the gym.

He met her as she walked in the door.

"Would you dance with me please, Laura?" he asked.

She looked into those blue eyes and forgot her resolve.

He took her hand and she stepped into his arms and it felt like she was in heaven or in a dream or something. It was just like in the romances. The music was all around them, and there was no one else but them. She could feel his hand burning her back and his chin brushing her hair and the rough feel of his suit against her cheek. She closed her eyes. She smelled the fragrance of his after-shave, felt his breath in her hair, felt him step to the music. And she couldn't move. When he stopped, she was mortified.

"I can't dance with you," she said. She tore herself away from him and ran from the dance floor.

Chapter Five

Michael studied the jumble of pins on the wall of his office. What a tedious way to make up a timetable. Most schools did their scheduling by computer, but not Providence. Mr. Walsh had been juggling colored pins for twenty-eight years, and he did not see any need for change. "It's good for you," he had told Michael. "It keeps you sharp. Not only that, but by the time you're through, you know where everyone is, what they're doing, and why."

"There's enough to keep me sharp just running this school," Michael had told him. "If I had known I'd be stuck playing trial and error with colored pins, I would have searched out an appropriate computer program. Let the computer run through all the permutations and combinations—that's what computers do best."

"You're not complaining, are you?"

"No, no." He couldn't complain. Principal of Providence School was a pretty fantastic promotion, especially after only eleven years of teaching experience.

The promotion had been sudden. When the superintendent of schools had suffered a heart attack, Mr. Walsh, as the senior administrator in the district, became the new superintendent. His old position was advertised, but Michael hadn't thought to apply.

The call from Mr. Walsh came as a surprise. "Michael," his voice boomed through the telephone. "Have you sent in your résumé?" And then, not waiting for a reply, he had continued, "It's already Wednesday and applications close at noon on Friday. You'd better get cracking and submit."

So Michael had applied. There wasn't enough time to mail his application, so he hand-delivered it to the board office just before the deadline. A few days later, three school board members and the new superintendent of schools, Mr. Walsh, interviewed him for the position. By the next Friday, the job was his.

He should be happy to have the chance to do the timetable no matter how tedious or old-fashioned the task. There had to be a technique to it. Michael thought of calling Mr. Walsh and asking for help, but that wasn't his style.

So he gritted his teeth and juggled pins. Classes, courses, time slots, and teachers had to be plotted on a grid. Each teacher had been assigned a color. The object of the activity was to mark each of the squares with one of the colored pins, ending up with no empty squares and no leftover pins. It sounded simple—but it wasn't.

Laura Hart. He picked up a red pin. Red for temper, red for her little red car, red for . . .

Michael walked to the window and stared out at the parking lot. This time next week, the lot would be full. Today, it was empty except for two vehicles—his van and the caretaker's truck. And maybe Laura's little sports car would come and fill one of the spaces.

She had said that she would be in today, but it was almost noon and there was still no sign of her. The conversation in front of Providence Foods had gone relatively well.

Why wasn't she here? Was it possible that she was still rebelling? Surely she had outgrown all that!

In her senior year, he had seen two very different sides to her. She had been a fun-loving organizer, very popular with the students, at the center of the crowd. She was the student council treasurer, an enthusiastic member of the cheerleading squad, and, seemingly, a go-getter who was involved in every activity that took place in the school. He knew she could write. She had written some very insightful articles for the school newspaper and given silly advice in the humorous, "Dear Prudence" column. However, in his class, she had submitted shoddy work and sometimes no work at all. She had often rushed through assignments or neglected to study for tests when other activities had interfered.

Michael had been short with her over the caliber of assignments she submitted. He knew she had talent and he had pushed her to use it. He had wanted her to be less frivolous. Perversely, the more he pushed, the more she balked. The result was that in his class, she had been totally irresponsible, and often flippant in her responses.

But from what he was told by the other teachers, that was the case only in his class. The others were pleased with her output. They had nothing but praise for Laura Hart.

He turned away from the window and went back to the timetable. He had too much to do, no time to waste watching for her. He scanned the columns but he couldn't concentrate. Thoughts of Laura kept intruding.

He listened to the steady tapping of Miss Peabody's typewriter in the outer office. It would take some doing to convince her to use a computer. In the eleven years since he had come to this town, he couldn't recall a single day that the secretary had missed. Lila Peabody lived a block from the school, and every morning, no matter what the weather and no matter what the circumstance, she could be counted on to be sitting at her desk, tapping away on the typewriter.

Was it possible that Laura was here? That she had walked to the school? That she had parked her car somewhere else? That she was here right now? Maybe she had gotten a ride into town, or maybe her car was at Sweeny's garage for a tune-up. Could she have made it past the office without him seeing her?

He dropped the red pin back into the little pin box on his desk and went into the outer office. "Miss Peabody," he asked, "have any of the teachers come in today?"

She continued typing, not missing a click. "If you mean Laura Hart," she said, "I haven't seen her today."

Michael was flustered. How did Miss Peabody know he was waiting for Laura? Was he that transparent? "Well, I think I'll go for a walk," he said. "I need to stretch my legs." He crossed the office past her desk and made for the door.

"Will you be gone long, Mr. Foster?"

"No, I'll be in the school," he called back, "the high school wing. Page me if you need me for anything."

In the darkened hall, the only light was what came through the classroom windows and spilled out the transoms and the open doors. The floors shone and everything smelled of lemon and bleach. There was a feeling of anticipation, of challenge, like before the start of a big game. Michael loved it.

He automatically gravitated toward his old classroom, at the end of the hall. The door was open; he looked in. The room was empty.

He entered and for a long while he stood just inside the door, savoring the calm and comfort it brought. It felt good to be there. This had been his territory for the past eleven years. A territory where, for the most part, he had been successful and happy. How many students had he taught in this very room?

He walked around the room, savoring the memories. The desks had seen many years and many students, but they looked in surprisingly good condition. They had been scrubbed clean of last year's doodles. Only the messages which had been scratched into the paint or carved into the wood remained.

One desk read, "School sucks."

He wondered who had scratched that message into the metal rail. "I'm sorry kid. I hope it was just a bad day for you. You must have had some good days, too."

"JD + BT" was written on a desk. Which made him smile.

"RW slept here". Rick's desk. That was two years ago. Rick used to doze off almost every day after staying up most of the night watching television.

"BB loves LH". Bobby Berent loves Laura Hart.

Laura's desk. Michael remembered when he scolded her for carving up her desk. She had looked him in the eye and said nothing. A couple of days later, Mary had come to tell him that he shouldn't have accused Laura of vandalizing her desk, that it was Bobby who had done the carving.

Michael had tried to apologize to Laura, but she had given him a frosty look. As a result, his apology came through gritted teeth. Irritation had been a fact of life when he dealt with Laura.

It was her room now.

As he looked around at the posters and pictures that gave life to the bulletin boards, he was impressed by the little touches that made this room hers.

He went to the teacher's desk, sat in the old oak chair, leaned his elbows on the well-worn desk, and allowed himself to reminisce.

Laura had sat in the row near the windows, in the third desk from the front. She had been in his morning class.

"Mr. Foster," Miss Peabody's voice commanded over the intercom. "There's a telephone call for you, Mr. Foster."

"I'm on my way," he called out to the voice box by the door.

"Michael." The voice on the line was that of Mr. Walsh. "Thought I'd check to see how you're doing."

Michael liked Mr. Walsh. "I'm sweating over that relic you call a timetable," he grumbled. "Other than that, I'm fine."

Mr. Walsh chuckled. "Good. A little sweat never hurt. I'm glad you're staying out of trouble."

Michael laughed. "I'm trying. How are you enjoying your new job? Are you busy enough, or are you going to come and help me get this show on the road?"

"There's a blizzard of paper on my desk," Mr. Walsh said. "Not to worry, we'll both do fine. By the way, have you had a chance to talk to any of the teachers yet?"

"Not really. Most are still away on their holidays."

"What about Laura Hart? Has she been in yet?"

Michael kept his voice casual. "Laura Hart is the new English teacher," he said. "Yes, she was in yesterday."

"But you never saw her."

"Yes, I saw her . . . yesterday."

"Anything wrong, Michael?"

"No, no. She seems very capable. Eager to start."

"Good. Laura's a bright girl. She has a lot to offer the school, but I'm sure you remember her, don't you?"

"Yes, I do."

"You're not saying much, Michael. Does that mean you think she's going to be a problem for you?"

"Why do you ask?"

"I remember the year she was in your class. It seems to me that you two had some differences of opinion. I hope that's not going to be the case this year."

"We won't have a problem," Michael was quick to reply. "It was my first year. I was young. Laura was popular and powerful. I think what we had, was a bit of a power struggle. Unfortunately, I was too inexperienced to know how to handle her."

Mr. Walsh laughed. "You were green, all right, and you sure didn't bend much. You took yourself so seriously that you kind of set yourself up. A strong-minded student like Laura had no trouble at all finding buttons to push."

"By the way," Michael changed the subject, "we're short some supplies. I was looking at last year's requisitions. Unless I'm reading them wrong, there should be a few boxes coming our way. Any idea when we can expect them?"

"There's a truck coming out to the school on Thursday. Most of your order should be on it."

They talked a little longer.

Finally, Mr. Walsh advised Michael to "lighten up a little and let yourself have a good year."

The conversation ended. Michael stared at the telephone and wondered just exactly how he was supposed to lighten up.

He noticed the binders on his shelf. They were full of lesson plans and work sheets that he had used in his teaching. The spine of one big red binder had the words "English 30 (gr. 12)" printed on it in black felt marker. A big blue binder was labeled "English 20 (gr. 11)" and the green one said "English 10 (gr. 10)".

He opened the red binder. The whole course was there. He had prepared it in his first year, but then revised and fine-tuned it each year for the past ten years. He had gathered additional information, prepared work sheets, assignments, test questions, project suggestions.

Now that he was the principal, he would no longer need the notes. Laura would be the one teaching the English courses this year. She might find the materials useful. It certainly wouldn't hurt to help her out a little.

He went to the storage room and found an empty cardboard box. Returning to his office, he filled the box with the binders of notes and whatever else he could find that pertained to the subjects she would be teaching. He might as well let her have it all. With three new courses to teach, surely she would appreciate his help. She might even begin to defrost a little.

Laura? Appreciate anything he did? Not likely. She'd probably find some reason to be offended. She had called him arrogant. Would she see this as another example of his arrogance?

She'd have to, at least, appear to bury the hatchet somewhere other than in his skull. Michael smiled to himself. It might be fun to watch her reaction.

He set the box by the door, went back to his work, and waited for her to arrive. But what if she didn't come? Then he'd just have to drive out to her farm and deliver the box to her.

Michael knew where Laura lived. He had driven past the Hart farm many times on his way to a special fishing hole. A couple of times a month, at least, Michael found peace as he stood alone on the riverbank, watching the water splashing over a series of gentle rapids, then swirling and eddying past two protective boulders to calm itself in the basin where fish congregated in the deep water before continuing downstream. The sound of the water combined with the slow rhythm of his rod, casting and reeling, casting and reeling, helped him to relax. This is where he did his best thinking. And most days he managed to catch a fish for his supper.

Michael had discovered the fishing hole in the spring of his first year in Providence. Old Man Martin's place. His own special place. He had never seen anyone else there. There was no reason for him to stay in Providence, and as a matter of fact, a city would have provided more opportunities for him, but along with his attachment to the community, the fishing hole probably had a lot to do with keeping him there.

At the end of Michael's first year, he got a call from Rick, one of his friends from the university. "How would you like to go north this summer? I got a new Jeep—four-wheel drive. It can go anywhere."

It sounded good.

Rick went on, "My dad's got a tent and a cooler and a camp stove he's not planning to use. All we need is sleeping bags."

"I might be interested," Michael had told him. "Depends how long you want to take."

"We've got all summer."

"I don't know about all summer." Michael hesitated.

"We can take a canoe, our fishing rods—come on, Michael, it would be heaven," Rick said. "I don't know about you, but this past year was pretty darned exhausting."

"It really sounds good, but I've got to think about it, okay. I was kind of planning to stay in Providence, run a basketball camp."

"You've got to be crazy to stick around when you don't have to."

"Maybe I am crazy, but I'll tell you what, Rick," he said. "You help me run the camp and I'll come with you for a month."

On his way back into town, he stopped at Sweeny's for gas. Bobby Berent's truck was parked by the garage door. He was squatting beside it, putting air in his tires.

"Hi, coach," Bobby called.

"What's happening, Bobby?" Michael asked. "Why the frown?"

"Nothing's happening."

"You don't look so happy. Is everything okay?"

"Laura's gone," Bobby said.

"What do you mean, gone?"

"She just up and left." Bobby walked around to the other side of his truck to check the tires.

Michael got out of his van and went over to talk to him. "Did she say where she was going?"

"She said she was going to the university, but everybody knows it doesn't start till September."

"Maybe she just needed to get away for a while. She'll probably be back in a few days."

"Are you gonna be leaving too?" Bobby asked.

"No, I'm staying."

"You were a good teacher," Bobby said. "I liked it on your team."

"I'm thinking of running a basketball camp this summer."

"That's great."

"If I do, would you like to help?"

"You bet. As long as it's not during harvest. I've got to help my dad with the combining."

"How about the first two weeks of August? That should be okay for most students, don't you think? I'm going to run it by Mr. Walsh and see what he thinks."

By the time Michael left, Bobby was grinning from ear to ear.

Mr. Walsh was enthusiastic. "It's an excellent idea, Michael. The school's empty all summer anyway. May as well get some use out of it," he said. "We'd better get the word out real soon, if you're serious."

"I am serious," Michael said.

"Haven't you got anything better to do?"

"I'll be doing some wilderness camping in July, but I'd like to work with the kids in August."

"You're quite a guy," the principal said.

"Providence has been good to me."

Chapter Six

Laura poured her mother another cup of tea. It seemed that tea was all her mother wanted these days. Laura tried a variety of soups and juices, but her mother hardly touched them.

"It's nice having you back home," Mrs. Hart said. She took a sip. "We've missed you these past few years."

"I missed you too, Mom."

"I don't understand why you stayed away for so long."

"I'm grown up now. I've got my own life." Laura went to the sink and rinsed out the teapot. "You can't expect me to live at home and be your little girl forever."

"I guess not," her mother said. "It used to be so nice when you all were little. There was always talk and laughter in this house. You kids used to keep us hopping. Now, with all of you gone and Dad out in the field, the only talk and laughter I hear is on the TV."

"Well I'm home now, Mom," Laura consoled.

"Too bad school starts so soon. Just a couple more days and you're going to be gone all the time."

Laura hated it when her mother talked that way. Mrs. Hart had always been so cheerful, but since her illness, she had more and more bad days. Her depressions seemed much more frequent.

"Don't worry, we'll have plenty of time together, Mom," she said. "But I really like teaching. I'm looking forward to being in the classroom again."

"I don't think you're going to be happy teaching here," her mother said.

"Sure I will, Mom. Why shouldn't I be happy teaching here?"

"Now they've got this new principal," her mother said.

"What about the new principal?"

"He was your teacher, wasn't he? Wasn't he the one that made you so miserable? You didn't have much to say about him that was any good."

"He wasn't that bad. I was more than partly to blame," she said. This was a switch. She was defending Michael.

"I just hope he treats you better than he did when you were in high school. I don't want to see you coming home all upset again," her mother continued.

Laura finished wiping the kitchen counter. "Don't worry, I won't come home upset."

Shep gave a few friendly barks to announce Bobby's arrival, and then Bobby was on the front step, talking to the dog. "How are you doing Shep, old boy?"

Laura's mother cheered up. "Bobby's here."

He banged on the screen door, opened it, stuck his head in the house, and shouted, "Hey, Laura, you ready?" It was just like old times.

"Come on in," she called out.

"Hello, Mrs. Hart," he greeted. "How's my favorite neighbor lady?"

"Oh, you big tease," Laura's mother giggled.

It was nice to see her mother cheerful. Bobby was just what her mother needed. He certainly could charm her back to health if anybody could.

"Smells like vinegar around here. What is this, some new city-type perfume you brought back with you?"

"We've been putting pickles in jars," she said. "You've come just in time to tighten the lids."

Bobby picked up a jar, tightened its lid, and winked at Laura's mother. "She needs me. I'm indispensable."

Laura groaned. "Are you ever in good form this afternoon. You must have practiced your wisecracks all night."

"Admit it, Laura. You can't live without me."

"Just get busy with those jar lids."

"She's just as bossy as she ever was. We'd better keep her away from the vinegar."

Laura tossed a dishtowel at him.

"Help!"

Mrs. Hart smiled at Bobby. "That's what we need around here. We need you to lighten up the mood."

Bobby certainly had lightened up the mood. Her mother's eyes were sparkling, and her talk was animated.

Laura wished things were different. If only she could love Bobby. Life would be so much simpler, so much better for everyone concerned. For everyone?

Her mother was chatting with Bobby. "She's been working all morning, picking and cleaning vegetables. You should see how many packages of green and yellow beans she put into the freezer. She'll make some man a great wife."

Laura felt impatient. She hated it when her mother extolled her rather dubious virtues as though she wasn't there. "You're supposed to be resting, Mom."

"I will, dear," Mrs. Hart said sweetly. All signs of her previous depression were gone as she turned her attention to Bobby. "I just want to chat with my favorite young man."

Bobby tightened another jar. "You just keep reminding her how wonderful I am, Mrs. Hart. I need all the help I can get."

Laura's mother beamed at him.

He gave her a conspiratorial wink, then turned to Laura and gave her an exaggerated leer. "You are looking awfully good but you'd better change your clothes," he said, indicating the white shorts and T-shirt she was wearing. "You don't want to get grease on those."

"I think she's gotten too thin. I don't think she looked after herself very well up there. Just work, work, work."

"Mother . . ."

"You'll have her fattened up in no time." Bobby was obviously enjoying himself.

Laura gritted her teeth. "I'm going right now," she said, hurrying out of the kitchen before she said something unpleasant to her mother.

She shut her bedroom door and leaned against it, feeling guilty. What the heck was wrong with her? She should be more patient with her mother. Her mother meant no harm. She had to stop overreacting, but for some reason—maybe it was habit—she couldn't help herself.

Laura found an old pair of blue jeans and stepped into them. They still fit. She pulled a baggy old shirt over her head without bothering to undo the buttons.

With her mother so ill, surely it wouldn't hurt to humor her. But darn it all, she resented her mother's constant efforts to pawn her off on Bobby. At times it was all Laura could do to watch her tongue.

Working in the garden all morning had been pure pleasure. It reminded her of when she was just a little girl, not yet in school. She had her own little garden plot right beside her mother's. She had sprinkled a whole package of mixed flower seeds there, and every day she went out with her little watering can and watered her garden. The flowers had been remarkable. Even her sister and brother had said so.

Laura's sister and brother were ten and eleven years older than she was. They went off to school, but even when they were at home, they didn't want her chasing along after them. So whenever she was allowed, Laura had tagged along with her father. She had helped him feed chickens, watched him throw bales of hay to the cows, handed him tools when he repaired machinery, and pounded nails into anything that would take them.

When she started school, she and Bobby rode the bus together and soon were spending much of their time together, usually outside, helping his father or helping hers.

She loved the farm. Here, she had felt creative, free—except for her senior year. That was when she saw the chute and knew that unless she took off, she would be herded right into it.

This morning, Laura had felt the old freedom, and this afternoon, she had felt satisfaction at the little packages and jars she had created. But now, she was beginning to feel trapped again, just like she had felt before she'd left home.

She did not need, or want, to be auctioned off to the highest bidder—or any bidder, for that matter. Was that so hard for her mother to understand?

She tied her hair back into a ponytail and pulled on a pair of socks. She should have gone back to school this morning. By staying home, she had inadvertently fueled her mother's hopes. She would just have to dampen them. But her mother was very sick—she might not even last the year. Shouldn't she try to keep her happy? But at what cost? She stepped into a pair of sneakers and tied the laces, put on a smile, and then came back out to where Bobby and her mother were still enjoying their conversation.

An hour later, as she perched up on the top of the combine, Laura's anger was forgotten. She was grubby and sunburned but she felt great.

"Sure is hot today." Bobby looked up at her and wiped the perspiration off his face with his sleeve. "I could use a cold drink right about now."

"There's soda in the fridge up at the house," Laura replied. "Do you want to take a break?"

"Nah, I'm almost done." He picked up the grease gun and walked around the big machine, giving a shot here, another shot there.

Shep, who had been sleeping beside the combine, suddenly jumped up and, barking furiously, ran toward the road.

A blue van, followed by a plume of dust, was pulling into the yard. She knew who it belonged to. She had seen it in the school parking lot. But what was he doing here? Her breathing stopped, and she had a strange buzzing sensation in her ears. Was it stage fright?

She saw him climb out of the vehicle, and for a moment, fear gripped her as she watched Shep bound toward him. Michael said something to the dog, then crouched down to make friends with him. She could see Shep's tail wagging furiously as Michael petted him. Then Shep rolled over and let Michael scratch his stomach. She couldn't believe it.

Her throat was tight. What did he want? He'd obviously come looking for her. What should she do?

She looked down at her grubby shirt. She couldn't go and talk to him, not looking like this. She finger-brushed the hair off her face, then retied her ponytail. The best thing to do was to pretend she didn't know he was here.

Bobby came out from behind the combine. "Hey, Laura, look who's here. It's the coach!" he said.

Laura watched as Michael, accompanied by a surprisingly friendly Shep, went to the house. Her mother would send him out here to see her. Please, no, not today!

"I wonder what he's doing here?" Bobby voice was puzzled.

"How would I know?" She was brusque in her response.

Bobby gave her a curious look. "Hey, don't get mad at me."

"I'm sorry," she said. "He's the new school principal. That makes him my boss, and that's probably why he's here."

"Yeah, I heard he was the principal now. Maybe he's here to tell you you've been fired," Bobby joked.

She was in no mood for Bobby's jokes. She watched Michael as he came from the house, expecting him to come her way, but instead of heading toward the combine, he returned to his van, opened the side door, and took out a large cardboard box.

"Looks like he's bringing you something," said Bobby.

"Oh, no!" Laura moaned as she watched Michael take the box to the house. "You're right. He brought back all of my stuff. I can't believe it."

"Believe what?"

"I've been fired!"

"I was just kidding when I said that, Laura." Bobby was looking at her strangely. "Where's your sense of humor? Of course you haven't been fired."

Why couldn't Bobby understand? It was as obvious as obvious could be. "Me and my big mouth!"

"What are you talking about?"

"I shouldn't have mouthed off yesterday, but he just made me so mad," she explained.

"So you mouthed him off, so what's new? The coach wouldn't make a big thing of it. He isn't like that."

"You know he always hated me."

"No, he didn't hate you. You were the one who was always mad at him. He couldn't do anything right as far as you were concerned. I don't understand why you were like that."

"So now you think it was my fault! He was the one who always picked on me."

"Yeah, and no wonder! You were something else

that last year. There were times when you really deserved it."

Laura was furious with Bobby for defending Michael. "Don't you dare take his side, Bobby Berent!"

"I'm not taking his side."

"If your precious coach is firing me, you'd think he'd have the guts to tell me to my face, wouldn't you?"

"Take it easy, Laura," Bobby cautioned. "Don't go jumping to conclusions."

Laura climbed down the little ladder. "No, I'm not going to take it easy, and I'm not jumping to conclusions," she fumed. "I'm going over there and I'm going to see if he's got the guts to tell me to my face. Let him explain why it is he's letting me go." She strode up the driveway to where Michael had just opened the door to his vehicle.

"Mr. Foster!" she called out.

Michael went to meet her. "You're here," he said. "I was just talking to your mother. She said you weren't at home."

"Well I am," she replied. A tendril of hair had loosened itself from her ponytail and was tickling her cheek. As she brushed it away with the back of her hand, she left yet another smudge mark on her face. She was wonderful; she was a mess. She looked like an auto mechanic—no, a grease monkey. Her face, hands, and clothes were all smeared with dirt and grease.

Michael's initial reaction was to laugh, and when he realized that the expression on her face was anything but friendly, he couldn't resist the urge to tease her, "You are a woman of many talents, Laura. Can I get you to give my van a tune-up."

She looked him straight in the eye. "Mr. Foster," she said, her voice icy. "You didn't come out here to make small talk. To what do I owe the pleasure of this visit? Will you tell me or do I have to get the message secondhand from my mother?"

What the heck was going on? "You weren't at school so I decided to bring you some books."

She stood by the side of the driveway with her arms at her sides. Michael noticed that she kept well away from him and that her hands were clenching and unclenching as she replied, "Thank you for sparing me the trip."

Michael gazed up at the sky and scratched his head in puzzlement. There was no doubt about it, she was mad. He wondered what he had done to set her off this time. There was no apparent reason for her to be so chilly—after all he had just done her a favor. "No problem," he said. "I was heading this way anyway."

She nodded and stepped back, dismissing him.

Behind her, Michael could see that someone was by the combine, looking their way. The man looked familiar. "Is that Bobby Berent down there?"

"Yes, it is."

Bobby just stood there watching them. Michael waved and Bobby waved back.

So that was why she was icy. She had something going with the Berent boy and didn't want him hanging around, wrecking things. "How's it going, Bobby?" he called out.

"Good, how about you?"

"Good too." Seeing them here together reminded Michael of the way things had been. Laura and Bobby had always been part of the same group. They had been the popular kids—the athletes, the student council, the club leaders.

"I'd better go. Sorry to have disturbed you and your boyfriend," he said.

"Good-bye," she replied, still frosty.

He felt a sinking sensation. What was the use? He couldn't let her know how he felt, and maybe it was just as well. She obviously loved Bobby and just as obviously, she hated him.

"See you at school."

"At school?" She looked surprised, almost as if he had said something she hadn't expected to hear.

"Will you be in tomorrow?" he asked. He still wanted to see her, even if it was hopeless.

"Tomorrow? You want me to come in? What for?" She was looking at him in a puzzled way. He wondered what the heck he had said or done.

"Well if you do, I'll be seeing you."

She looked uncertain.

He went back to his van and slid the side door shut. He had no idea what was going on. He felt as though he had stepped into the twilight zone. He went around to the driver's side, climbed in, and started the engine.

She followed him around to his side of the vehicle. He rolled down the window. "I hope you find the books helpful," he said. He felt that the conversation hadn't really ended, that he should say something more.

She was no help. She stood watching him with those big dark eyes and said nothing. He waited for her to speak.

She didn't.

Michael backed the van, turned, and drove out of the yard. What was the use!

As he drove away, he noticed in the rear-view mirror that she was still standing there, watching after him. He waved, and she raised her hand in what could have passed for a wave.

With an empty feeling in his chest, he turned toward town.

Chapter Seven

It was mid-morning when Laura drove into the schoolyard. Michael's van was there, as was the caretaker's truck. She parked her car at the far end of the lot, as far as possible from Michael's office window. After the reception she had given him yesterday afternoon, she wasn't looking forward to facing him.

She could feel her face heating up with embarrassment when she remembered the way she had treated him. How could she possibly have known that the reason he had come out to see her was just to be helpful? He certainly had never given any indication that she could expect kindness from him, at least not that she could recall.

A niggling doubt made her stomach uneasy. Okay, so maybe she was exaggerating. Maybe he hadn't treated her that badly, but she wanted to stay angry with him. She needed to justify her impossible behavior.

It had been only natural for her to think he was bringing back her belongings. After all, it wasn't Michael who hired her—it was Mr. Walsh. And from what Michael knew of her, it would be pretty unlikely that he would. She had not been an impressive scholar in his class. And as for her temperament... No, he probably wouldn't expect her to be a good teacher. He would certainly not have hired her.

As far as keeping her on staff, Michael had never liked her very much, and to top it all, she had been disrespectful and argumentative. He would have been within his rights to give her her walking papers. She would have understood.

Whose side am I on?

What she didn't understand was why she didn't keep her mouth shut, why she never kept her mouth shut around Michael. Even the most stupid person in the world would have had more sense that to mouth off the boss, especially more than once, and especially before the job even started.

But she always overreacted when Michael was around. For some reason, with him she became irrational. She had been mortified when she discovered that, once again, she had put her foot in her mouth where he was concerned.

She reached across to the passenger seat for the books and her briefcase, opened the car door, and slid out. Casting a nervous glance at the office windows, she gently pushed the door shut. If she didn't let it slam, she might get into the building without being noticed.

She stole into the school on silent running shoes. Mr. Neil, the caretaker, was cleaning the trophy case in the main entrance. She inhaled the pine and lemon scent of the cleaning supplies, recognizing the smell that had greeted her as a student after every holiday. Even the cleaning supplies hadn't changed.

When he saw her, Mr. Neil put down the rag he was holding and came to greet her. "Welcome back," he said. "Do you need some help bringing your stuff in?"

She glanced down the hall to see if the main office door was open. "Thank you, Mr. Neil. I appreciate the offer, but I can manage," she replied, careful to keep her voice from carrying. "It's good to be back."

"Well, good luck to you. I hope you have a good year, and don't be shy to ask for help."

She smiled her appreciation and he went back to his work. Mr. Neil had been the caretaker when she was in high school but he didn't seem any older. The kids had all liked him. He never seemed to mind going on the roof to get a ball, or opening the classroom for some student who had forgotten his homework, or even cleaning up when someone had been sick. He was always cheerful, and he always had time and a good word for everyone.

As she passed the glassed-in main office area, she noticed that behind the secretary's desk, Michael's office door was closed. Luck was with her.

Miss Peabody looked up.

Laura smiled and nodded. She hurried past the office and down to the workroom. Then, groaning with relief, she deposited her armload of books on the workroom table and rubbed her aching arms to get the circulation going again.

The copy machine was by the back wall. It had been upgraded from the one she remembered, but it was a standard model—nothing complicated, thank heavens.

Laura went to the machine and turned it on. Then, while she waited for the copier to warm up, she organized the sheets she needed to reproduce.

As a student, she had not been allowed in the workroom except when she had worked on the school newspaper. One day each month, this had been the place where the newspaper had been printed, collated, and prepared for distribution.

She remembered the drawer where the supplies had been kept. She opened it and smiled to herself. Even in this room, very little had changed, she thought, as she took out a stapler and a paper punch.

The ready light on the machine came on, so she put in the first sheet, turned the counter to thirty-eight, and pushed the start button. According to Miss Peabody, she had thirty-six students on her class list. Plus one page for her and one for good measure.

Ten years ago, there were thirty-two students in the class. She wondered if there had been an increase in all the classes or if this was just a fluke.

When the first page was done, she copied the second page and then the third. While she waited for each of the pages to be printed, she busied herself preparing file folders.

Miss Peabody entered the workroom, and Laura quickly moved her papers to the side. "I've just finished with the machine," she said. "I only have to punch holes in the margins and staple a couple of pages, and then I'm out of here."

"As soon as I get this newsletter started, I'll give you a hand, if you'd like," Miss Peabody said.

Laura was surprised at the offer. Maybe the secretary wasn't so formidable after all. "Thank you for the offer, but I'll be fine. There's not much left to be done," she replied.

Miss Peabody piled a sheaf of bright yellow paper into the machine, put in the master sheet, set the number of copies, pushed the start button, and came to see what Laura was doing.

She picked up one of Laura's pages. "This looks like something I typed for Mr. Foster a while back."

"It probably is. Some of these sheets were originally his," Laura replied. "He gave them to me."

Miss Peabody took off her glasses and studied Laura with a look that most certainly meant disapproval.

Laura felt her blush returning. "It's because I have never taught these courses before. Mr. Foster was kind enough to let me use his notes and handouts."

"You don't have to explain anything to me," Miss Peabody said. She put on her glasses and went back to the copy machine. "What you do in your personal life is none of my business."

Laura didn't quite know how to respond, so she said nothing.

The copier reached the two hundred mark and stopped. The secretary took out the finished pages and set them on the table. She inserted the second master sheet, refilled the paper tray with the canary-colored paper, and, once again, pushed the button to restart the machine.

"He's a good man but he's too young," the secretary said. "He's going to have a tough year, coming up."

"I'm sure he'll do fine," Laura replied.

Miss Peabody shrugged her shoulders. "I hope he does. If he doesn't, we'll all know it." She picked up one of the staplers. "Shall I do these sheets?"

"Thank you."

"What he doesn't need is a whole lot of distractions."

Laura didn't reply. She wasn't sure what Miss Peabody was getting at, but she had a feeling that she was considered one of the distractions. She liked that feeling.

They worked in silence. When they finished Laura's papers, they worked together stapling the newsletter. On the first page was the principal's message welcoming back the students, teachers, and support staff, and a special welcome back to her as an ex-student who was now a teacher. Laura felt a lump in her throat. What would she have given for Michael to personally welcome her?

When the newsletters were done, Laura took her stack of papers and prepared to leave.

"Thank you for the help, Laura," Miss Peabody said. "If you want, I can type some of your tests and handouts."

This was the second offer of help from Miss Peabody. Laura was taken aback. She had never even expected the first offer. "Thank you," she said. "I appreciate the offer."

"All I need is a couple of days, so if you're not in a hurry, just leave the work on my desk and I'll do it when I have time." She gave Laura a kindly smile. "You'll do all right, Laura Hart. Don't you worry too much."

Back in her classroom, Laura felt at peace. Mr. Neil and Miss Peabody had made her welcome and offered their help. The room was warm and the sun was shining through the windows, giving a pleasant light. She set her stack of files she had prepared, on top of the filing cabinet and went back to sit at her old student desk. In this room, it still felt like hers—more so than the teacher's desk. The teacher's desk was indelibly Mr. Foster's.

Laura lay her cheek on her forearm and gazed out the window. Many times she had gazed out that window. The sky was baby blue with white fluffy clouds—a sky made for daydreams.

It was springtime, a beautiful May morning. There was only one more week until her eighteenth birthday, and graduation was just a few weeks after that.

The air was spring fresh and the crabapple tree outside her bedroom window was a mass of blooms. Laura felt alive.

The smell of freshly baked apple-cinnamon biscuits wafted into Laura's room. When she came into the kitchen, her father was sitting at the table, smearing butter on a biscuit.

"M-m-m, that smells so good, Mom. What's the occasion?"

"Molly Berent's coming over for coffee this morning. I decided to bake the biscuits early so you and your father could have some for breakfast," her mother said. "I know how much the two of you like my biscuits."

"You're a good woman, Helen," Laura's father said. He took a big mouthful of biscuit. "M-m-m. You sure know how to win a man's heart."

Laura's mother smiled. "You mean this is all it takes, just a couple of biscuits?"

Her father nodded. "You better learn from your mom, Laura. That way you'll know how to keep Bobby happy." He put the rest of the biscuit in his mouth.

"Bobby's just a friend, Daddy. That's all," she said. Her mother and father exchanged glances. They didn't believe her.

"Friendship's real important in a marriage, isn't that right dear?" her mother said.

Her father nodded. "You're going to have a real good life with Bobby, especially if you bake him some of these biscuits." He took another biscuit. "Man, these are good."

After she finished her breakfast, Laura got ready for school and went outside to enjoy the sunshine. Shep came to be petted, and she scratched him behind the ears. He was good company. Every day, he walked with her to the end of the lane and waited with her until the school bus arrived. And in the afternoon, when she came home from school, she always found him sitting there, waiting to walk with her back to the house.

It was still a little early for the school bus, so Laura and the dog took a walk around the yard. The fragrance of the blossoms on the little apple tree outside her bedroom window was intoxicating. Laura picked a few little branches of blossoms and took them in to her mother.

"Here you go, Mom. Some flowers for the table," she said.

"Thank you, dear. They're beautiful and they smell so nice. How about a sprig for you?" Her mother took the blossoms and pinned them in Laura's hair.

Laura caught the bus and forgot all about the flower.

She was sitting at her desk, reading a novel and waiting for the starting bell, when Michael entered the classroom.

He had obviously expected to find the room empty

because he seemed surprised to find her there. He had called her "a vision of spring," and she had felt all warm and tingly.

"They're apple blossoms," she had said, hoping for more.

"Of course," he said, but by now he had lost interest in the conversation. He sat at his desk and concentrated on the sheaf of papers in front of him.

Laura's chest had tightened so she had trouble breathing. She pretended to be reading her book, but all the while she watched him from the corner of her eye. She wanted him to look up, to look at her again, but he was too engrossed in his work.

Then the starting bell rang, and the sudden commotion in the halls spilled into the classroom.

That day, Laura couldn't stop smiling. A vision of spring, he had called her, a vision of spring.

Years later, that was one of the occasions Laura dwelled on. She played and replayed the scene, freeze-framing it. She locked into that simple remark, studying it, interpreting it, and savoring the sensation.

Michael did see Laura's car pull into the parking lot, and he noticed the distance she put between her car and his. That was a statement if there ever was one. Disappointed, he turned back to give the completed timetable a final check.

As far as any chance of making friends with Laura was concerned, there was none. He would be best off to stay away from her. Nevertheless, he found himself at her classroom door.

Laura was sitting in her old desk, in the row by the windows. The sun was glinting off her hair, creating an aura—angelic, untouchable. She was beautiful.

He did not want to disturb her, but she sensed his

presence, slowly raised her head, and looked his way with the distant expression of someone in a dream.

"Is everything okay?" he asked.

"This used to be my desk."

"I know," he said. He remembered the fiery little redhead, her head bent over a book or sketching a picture or earnestly arguing a point. She had loved fantasy and poetry. He had noticed the rapt expression on her face as he read to the class from Tennyson or Browning or Frost. He had tried to encourage her love of poetry, but with each of his attempts, she had feigned disinterest.

Laura's voice brought him back to the present. "I'm sorry I was so rude. I want to thank you for the all the notes you gave me. I found them very useful." She bit her lip, and he wondered if it was his presence that made her nervous. Or maybe she found it hard to say thank you.

"I'm glad they helped," he said. He wanted to enter the room, but he was rooted to the doorway.

"I've already made copies of some of your hand-outs," she said, leaving her desk. "Miss Peabody helped me staple them."

She moved in his direction. He felt like he did when he was hiking in the mountains and came upon a deer. It was her eyes. They were big and brown, so dark they looked almost black. He had a feeling that even the slightest move might spook her and cause her to run away. Michael held his breath.

She went to the filing cabinet, opened the top drawer, and began to file the folders that were sitting on top.

He watched her for a moment, her head bent over

the drawer, her hair a copper veil hiding her face. On impulse he asked, "Have you had lunch yet?"

She looked up at him.

Without waiting for an answer, he continued, "I was planning to go over to the cafe for a hamburger. I'd like you to come with me. What do you say?"

She looked as though she were considering the offer. Then she shook her head. "No, thanks. Maybe some other time."

He refused to take no for an answer. The thought of her sitting opposite him at lunch was too enticing. "I could use some company," he said.

She hesitated, so he pressed on. "Just a quick lunch. We'll walk over to the coffee shop, eat, and come right back. Half and hour, forty minutes tops."

"Well, all right," she said.

Chapter Eight

The Providence Cafe was a white stucco building two blocks from the school, so it was the logical place for all the young people to congregate. From September to June, the little coffee shop was filled with boisterous teenagers, both at the noon hour and after school. All year round, on Friday and Saturday nights, the high school's too-young-to-drink-liquor crowd met there. As a student, Laura had been a regular patron, but never with Michael. During the school year, when students filled the place, teachers avoided it.

When they got there, Michael held the door for her to go in ahead of him. She entered the coffee shop and immediately recognized the familiar booths with their red plastic seats and arborite tabletops and the arborite counter which still fronted the same red plastic stools. The only changes she perceived were several mismatched seats which had been re-covered with a different shade of red plastic.

This being August, the cafe was almost empty. "This place hasn't changed much has it?"

"Not very much," Michael replied. "Anywhere in particular you'd like to sit?"

"It doesn't matter," she replied. But then she saw the corner booth where she and her friends used to sit, and she gravitated toward it. "How about here?"

"Fine," Michael said as he followed her and slid into the bench across from her. "Was this your usual booth?"

She nodded.

They had come here after every home game—she and Bobby, Frank and Mary, Don and Susan, Brenda and Jake—and there were usually at least two or more of the others. And they had sat in this corner booth.

They had joked and laughed and made wisecracks. Don was the one who usually started them making music with their drinking glasses. Soon he had them all dipping their fingers in the water, then circling the rims of their glasses to make them hum.

Frank was the one who kept putting quarters into the jukebox. "Tonight's the Night!" was his favorite song. Then he used to sit with his arm around Mary. Sometime he had his hand on Mary's knee. The boys used to shout out the chorus and grin meaningfully at each other.

Mary didn't seem to mind.

But Laura sure did. She hated it when Bobby showed off like that with her. She remembered the time she had dug her nails into the back of Bobby's hand when he had patted her knee.

"Ouch! What did you do that for?" He had sounded surprised and a little resentful.

She had glared at him, and the guys had all laughed.

Bobby had blushed with embarrassment. "She just doesn't like me doing that in public," he'd said.

"I don't like you doing that at all."

The guys had exchanged looks that said they didn't believe her, and Laura noticed that Bobby didn't do anything to change their opinion.

"Tonight's the night!" they had all sung even louder.

Laura had thought it was just wishful bravado.

"Hi, Laura. Nice to see you back!"

Laura stared at the girl behind the counter. "Mary?"

The girl's hair was bleached and frizz-permed, and her smile was delighted as she came rushing over and threw her arms around Laura. "It's good to see you," she said. "It's been such a long time."

"It is Mary!" Laura hugged her back. "Oh, Mary, It's good to see you too," she said, and meant it. She wished she hadn't stayed away so long. "I was just thinking about you and the rest of the gang, and how we used to come in here all the time."

"Those were the good old days," Mary said. "Right, Michael?"

"Hi, Mary," Michael said. "How are you doing these days?"

She shrugged. "More of the same. But what about you? We hear you've been moved into Mr. Walsh's office. Congratulations. You'll make a good principal."

Michael thanked her.

Laura noticed how comfortable they were with each other and remembered how much his students had liked him.

"What are you doing back in town, Laura? How long are you here for?" Mary asked.

"I'm back to stay . . . for a while."

Mary squealed with delight. "That's great! We'll have to get together."

"That will be great," Laura agreed. "You can get me caught up on what everybody's doing. I haven't been gone that long, but I feel a little bit like a stranger."

"You?" Mary looked at Laura with wide-eyed amazement. "I can't imagine you feeling like a stranger. You were always in the middle of everything."

Laura smiled. "Maybe that's why. Since I've been back I've hardly seen anybody and been in the middle of nothing."

"You must have seen Bobby?"

Laura nodded.

"I'll bet he's happy you're back."

Laura tilted her head in agreement and glanced at Michael out of the corner of her eye. His expression remained unchanged. She felt frustrated. A while ago she had the impression that he wanted to be with her. Surely, if he was even slightly interested in her, he would be a little jealous of Bobby, or at least interested in the conversation.

"What can I get you?" Mary asked.

"A couple of hamburger platters," Michael said, eyeing Laura for confirmation. "Laura wants to see if they taste the same as they used to."

"They're a lot better, now that I'm cooking them," Mary said.

"I'll just have a plain hamburger and a chocolate

milkshake," Laura said. "I haven't had a good milk-shake since I left home."

"A milkshake sounds good. I'll have one too, but make mine strawberry," Michael said.

When Mary went off to prepare the drinks, Laura suddenly found herself at a loss for words. She glanced around the room, seeking a topic. "So you like strawberries," she said.

"My favorite fruit. What about you?"

"I like them too." There was a pause. "Do you come here very often?" she asked.

"Once in a while for a quick bite, when I'm too lazy to cook my own meal."

"I didn't know you could cook," Laura said. "That's silly, isn't it?"

Michael was looking at her with what appeared to be a twinkle in those devastating blue eyes of his. "Not at all," he said. "Most kids see their teachers as cyborgs that live in the school. They don't always realize that the teachers are human. They eat, sleep, live, love . . ."

Mary brought them the drinks. "There you go, chocolate and strawberry. Enjoy!" She placed the glasses in front of them and then she went back to the kitchen to prepare the hamburgers.

Laura sucked on her straw. She savored the rich chocolate drink and watched Michael enjoy his.

"You know something? It's been a long time since I had a milkshake," he said. "I didn't remember how good they were."

Laura nodded and sucked on her straw and waited for him to open the conversation. But Michael seemed quite content to sit there enjoying his drink and watching her.

She searched for a topic, a safe topic. "Everything's the same. As far as I can see, Providence even has the same number of cats and dogs it used to have."

"What did you expect? A city? You haven't been gone that long, you know. The population is pretty much the same, but there are half a dozen new houses on the west edge of town and a medical clinic opened up about a year ago."

"Why do you stay here?" she asked. "There can't be much for you to do here."

He looked into her eyes. "I like it here."

"I don't understand you. You're young and you could be anywhere else. I could see you staying here for a year or two," Laura said. "But this must be a boring place for someone like you. Everybody is either in school or married or old."

"You're not the first person to ask me what I see in this place." He thoughtfully stirred the straw around in his drink. "It's hard to explain. I like Providence. I like the people, I like the peacefulness of the country-side, the fields where the breezes promise freedom, the river. This is the kind of wholesome place where I can be at peace with myself, maybe do some good. I might even settle down here and raise a yard full of kids of my own someday."

Laura imagined herself with him and a yard full of kids and felt herself blush. Then, embarrassed at her reaction, she blushed even more.

Fortunately Mary arrived just then to serve them. "Business is a little slow. Mind if I join you two and hear what you're up to?"

"Please do." Michael moved into the booth to give Mary some room beside him. That brought him closer to Laura, a little closer than he needed to come. Laura was aware of his knee just inches from hers, and she had trouble concentrating on what Mary was saying.

"I hear your mom's been sick, Laura. How's she doing?"

"Some days she seems quite well, and other times not." Laura sighed. "All we can do is hope."

"So, that's why you're back."

Laura nodded. "That's why I'm back."

"There was talk that you and Bobby . . ."

Laura shook her head and reached for the ketchup bottle. She poured a large glob of the red sauce on her meat patty. "I've come to help at home. With Mom so sick and all the farm work and everything, it's just too much for my dad to handle all by himself."

"So you'll be staying for a while."

"Oh, yes. I'll be teaching here this year. But, what about you? You haven't told me anything about yourself."

"There's nothing to tell," Mary said. "I'm still here."

"I heard that you and Frank got married right away after we graduated."

"Yeah, we did. You knew I was pregnant?" Laura nodded and Mary continued, "Well, I lost the baby." There was catch in her voice.

"I'm sorry. I didn't know. I guess I kind of lost touch," Laura said, regretting her question. Poor Mary.

"When you left, you fell off the face of the earth." Mary sounded disappointed.

"I know. I couldn't help myself, I just had to get away, as far away as I could."

"But why?"

Laura shrugged. "I did come home Christmas most years, but by the time we had a big family meal and visited a little, it was time to go back. I never stayed long."

Mary was thoughtful. "You were smart to go off to school," she said. "Look at you now. You don't have to sling hash for minimum wage. You've got a good job."

Laura didn't know what to say, and Mary went on, "We all expected you and Bobby would have been married by now."

Again Laura shrugged. She didn't want to talk about Bobby, not in front of Michael. She wished Mary would let the topic go.

"Bobby's sure been faithful to you, you know," Mary said. "I don't think he's looked at another girl in all these years."

Laura noticed that Michael was watching her intently. She looked at her watch. "I've got to get back to work."

As they walked back to the school, Michael asked, "How is Bobby, anyway?"

"Bobby's the same as he always was," she replied.

Michael nodded. "He was a very likeable boy."

"He still is a likeable boy," she said.

"He's a man now."

"You liked all your students," Laura continued. "All except me."

He looked flustered. "I was young. Look, I'm sorry if you felt I disliked you. Believe me, I didn't and I don't. Quite the contrary."

It wasn't much, but Laura savored the remarks. What did he mean, quite the contrary?

Michael was flying high. The lunch with Laura had gone remarkably well. They had spent an entire hour together and hadn't argued even once.

It had been nice to see Laura so animated. She had certainly been happy to see Mary. Michael remembered them as always together, Frank and Mary and Bobby and Laura.

It was a good thing Laura got away from Providence. She might have ended up like Mary, worn out at twenty-eight.

Poor Mary.

Chapter Nine

Seven o'clock. Bobby would be arriving any minute to pick her up. Laura didn't really feel like going to a movie but she had promised. There was a lot of local news to catch up on, and Bobby had always been gabby. It would be just like old times. She'd have fun.

She wished it was Michael who was picking her up. She still couldn't believe that he had taken her out for lunch. It was hardly a date. She shouldn't get so excited about it. But they had talked and he said he liked her—well, he said he didn't dislike her, he said, quite the contrary.

Laura danced around the room, took her bottle of cologne, held it at arm's length, and waved it around as she pressed the button and sent a cloud of spray in her general direction.

No, she was silly to dream.

The dog's barking announced Bobby's arrival.

She quickly ran the brush through her hair and dabbed on a little lipstick.

There was a knock on her bedroom door, and then came her father's voice. "Laura, Bobby's here."

"I'll be right out." She took one last look in the full-length mirror—beige pants and a white knit top. She looked fine, but was her outfit too casual? She added a pair of big hoop earrings and a long gold chain. That should do it. After all, they were just going to see a movie, and no one dressed up for the movies any more.

She found Bobby in the living room, sitting in one of the armchairs and talking with her parents. Laura's mother was resting on the couch, propped up with pillows. Over her legs was a colorful afghan she had crocheted, and in her hands were the beginnings of another one. From the smile on her face, Bobby must have said something that had pleased her.

When Laura entered, Bobby immediately got up out of the chair and came to greet her. "Hi, Laura. Ready to go?"

Sweet Bobby! He had doused himself with spice-scented after-shave lotion, and his hair was slicked back and still damp. The white stripe on his forehead acknowledged the cap he always wore when he was out in the fields. In contrast, his complexion was ruddy from yet another sunburn and a thorough scrubbing with a powerful soap and a rough towel.

"I sure am," she replied.

"The second show's not till nine-thirty," Bobby said. "If we hurry, we've got time for Chinese food."

Laura hesitated. "Oh, Bobby, I'm not very hungry and I'm not dressed to go out for dinner."

He looked crestfallen. "I guess I should have said something sooner, eh?"

"Go on, Laura," her mother encouraged her. "You don't have to be hungry for Chinese food."

"And you're dressed up good enough. You look great to me," Bobby added.

Laura gave him a smile. What the heck, there was no reason to disappoint him. "Well then, let's go. By the time we get there I'll probably be hungry again. I'll just grab a sweater and my purse and I'll be ready to go."

Bobby gave her father the thumbs-up sign. Her father winked and returned it.

"What's all that about?" Laura asked.

The two men grinned at each other, and Laura was struck by how much they were alike—straightforward, honest, and dependable. Almost too honest, but this time she had the feeling they were up to something.

"Oh, nothing," her father said. "It's good to see that you still like food."

"Something is up," Laura said.

Her mother set the crocheting aside and got up off the couch. She gave Bobby a hug and he sheepishly hugged her back. "Good luck, son," she said in a loud whisper.

She turned to Laura, gave her a kiss on the cheek, and said, "You two have a good time, and don't rush home."

Laura sighed in resignation. "We're not going to be very late. We're coming home as soon as the show is over."

"What? You mean we're not going to go for hamburgers and fries before coming home? The city's ruined you," Bobby said.

"It's just I have lots of work to do tomorrow."

Later, in Bobby's truck, Laura said, "I'm sorry

about the way Mom's been pushing me at you. I wish she wouldn't keep putting you on the spot like that."

Bobby laughed. "I don't mind it at all. I can use all the help I can get when it comes to romancing you."

"We were best friends, Bobby. I'm going to a movie with my friend. That's really all it ever was. That's all it's ever going to be."

"You know what they say about friends?"

"What?"

He grinned at her. "Good friends make great partners."

"Don't get your hopes up. I'm not planning to settle down for a long, long time."

"Then I'm going to be waiting a long, long time."

"Please don't, Bobby." Laura felt a sick lump in the pit of her stomach. Why couldn't life be simple? Why did good people have to get hurt? Why couldn't she love Bobby the way he wanted?

And why couldn't Michael love her?

"Hey," he interrupted her thoughts. "Cheer up. I was going to ask you to marry me, but if it scares you, I'll wait and ask you tomorrow."

"Please, don't ask me, Bobby. You won't like the answer."

"I'm not saying we should get married right away. I just want it to happen someday."

"There was nobody whose company I enjoyed more. I loved hanging around with you. We had some really good times. Why can't we just stay friends?"

"We belong together, Laura. It's exactly because we are friends. We get along real good. That's why I know we're right for each other." He was so earnest. How could she make him understand without hurting him?

"We'd have to be more than friends to have a happy

marriage, Bobby," she said. "I just don't love you the way you want me to."

"We could be happy together, Laura. I know it and you'd know it too if you weren't so stubborn."

Laura shook her head. "I don't want to talk about that any more, okay, Bobby? Let's talk about something else."

"Like what?"

"Like . . . how are the crops looking?"

"Okay, we'll talk about crops," he said. "They're good this year, really good. We had some early rain that gave them a good start, and it was a nice hot summer. Yep, the crops are good."

There was a long silence.

Laura broke the silence. "So, what have you been up to this past year?"

"This year I've been busy on the farm. But the last few years I've helped the coach run some basketball camps."

"You helped coach basketball? I bet you enjoyed that."

He nodded. "Sure did."

She suddenly remembered what Michael had said. "Oh, that reminds me. Michael, I mean Mr. Foster, asked me to tell you that he could use some help coaching this winter. He said for you to let him know if you're interested."

"You bet I'm interested." Bobby looked like a happy kid.

"How did it ever come about that you got so involved with coaching basketball?"

"It happened right after you left. I was feeling down and the coach tried to cheer me up. He asked me to help, and I said okay. We had a good time and the kids sure liked it too."

"So you and Mi—Mr. Foster got along pretty well?"

"Oh, yeah, he's a great guy," he said. They drove on in silence for a few minutes. "Hey, did you know that Old Man Martin's living in Lethbridge now, and his place is up for sale?"

"That was a pretty place. With all those trees and the river, and that pond."

"Don't talk about the pond. Frank and I nearly froze. I've never liked swimming since then."

"Remember how we used to sneak over and steal crabapples off his tree?" she said. "Poor old guy. He was strange. We were all scared of him."

"Yeah. He got stranger and stranger. Turned into a real hermit. His place is so run down, I doubt anyone will buy it."

The time passed quickly and Laura began to relax again, so that by the time they pulled in front of the restaurant, her tension was completely gone and she was looking forward to the evening.

Bobby switched off the engine, reached across, and gave Laura's hand a squeeze. "Come on, let's go and eat. We're going to have a good time tonight."

Michael was in the restaurant with Sheila. He looked across the table at her. She was everything a man could want—beautiful, intelligent, and what's more, she was pleasant company. Why then was he so restless?

He had been seeing Sheila for the past six months, but the relationship wasn't going anywhere. She was the latest in a series of women he had dated in the last few years, but none of them had lasted very long.

He had been searching for a meaningful relationship, but each time the crucial ingredient was missing.

Although he had liked all of the women he had dated, none had caused him to fall in love. With Sheila, it was no different than it had been with any of the others. It was time to break it off.

Sheila interrupted his thoughts, "When are you going to leave that little hick town, Michael? You know that there are job openings in the cities. It would be so much better for your career, not to mention your social life, if you moved to a city—any city."

She had asked him that question almost every time they had been together—more so in the last few months. It was a legitimate question. He wondered about it himself, so it surprised him to hear himself say, "I think I may just stay in Providence for the next few years. Maybe settle down there."

"But Michael, why would you do that?" She looked disappointed. "It's so far from anywhere."

"Maybe that's its appeal," he said. "I grew up in cities, moving every time my father got another promotion. That's not for me. I want the simple life."

"Won't you get tired of it?"

"Maybe, but I'll cross that bridge if and when I come to it. For now, I'm happy." He took a mouthful of ginger beef. He liked the hot, spicy flavor. He caught himself thinking of Laura. She was anything but bland.

Almost as if on cue, Laura and Bobby entered the restaurant.

Michael observed the proud and possessive way that Bobby escorted Laura to a table, and suddenly his food became tasteless.

"Michael, is something the matter?" his date asked.

He tore his eyes away from the couple and and back to her. "No, nothing's the matter. What makes you ask?"

From the corner of his eye, he noticed that Bobby had spotted him and was pointing him out to Laura.

"Those people seem to know you," Sheila said. "Do you know who they are?"

"Which people?"

"By the door. They're coming this way."

"Oh, them," Michael said. "Yes. They're from Providence." Laura had a slight frown, but Bobby was grinning broadly. He returned Bobby's big grin with a smile of greeting as Bobby guided a seemingly reluctant Laura to his table.

"Hey, coach! Long time no see!" Bobby held out his hand.

"Hello, Laura, Bobby." Michael stood and shook hands with Bobby. He wanted to take Laura's hand but she ignored the move.

Laura gave Michael a brief smile and, keeping her hands at her sides, turned to greet his date.

"Laura, Bobby," Michael said. "Sheila."

There were general "pleased to meet you's." Michael noted that Bobby was the only one who appeared to be sincere. Laura seemed remote. Sheila was chilly.

"Why don't you join us?" he invited.

Laura shook her head. "No thank you."

Michael knew it was foolish, but he wanted them to stay. So did Bobby. He pulled out a chair for Laura next to Michael. "Come on, Laura, let's join them. I haven't seen the coach in a long time."

"Please," Michael said. Laura sat down.

"Laura told me you wanted me to help with the team."

"I sure could use you. I still plan to coach, but there are bound to be times when I can't be there. It would help if I could depend on you to carry on without me if necessary."

"Okay. You can count me in."

Sheila was looking at Bobby and Laura, sizing them up. "So you two are from Providence."

"Yeah, we are." Bobby beamed her a smile.

The waiter came and took their order.

"That must be a pretty special town. I can't seem to tear Michael away from it," Sheila said.

"It's a good town. We like it," Bobby said proudly. He sat on the other side of Michael, across from Laura. "By the way, coach, congratulations on making principal." He clapped Michael on the shoulder.

"Thanks. More than congratulations, what I need is for you to wish me luck."

"Good luck, then. You'll do a good job of it. We all thought you were a real good teacher, didn't we, Laura?" He asked for corroboration.

Laura nodded in assent, and Michael replied, "Thanks again."

"Boy, you gave Laura a scare when you came out to the farm." Bobby grinned conspiratorially at Michael.

"How's that?" He sent Laura a questioning look.

"She thought you were going to fire her." Bobby chuckled.

"Fire her?" Michael noticed that Laura was trying to look indifferent, but the blush that was creeping up her neck gave away her embarrassment.

Michael laughed aloud. "Did you really think I was going to fire you?"

Laura shrugged. "It crossed my mind."

"What on earth for?"

"I don't want to talk about it, okay?"

"I can't fire anybody, or hire anybody for that matter. That's not part of my job description. But why did you think I'd want to fire you?"

"I said, I don't want to talk about it."

Before Michael could comment, Sheila interrupted their conversation. "Were you one of Michael's students?" she asked Laura. He noticed that her voice held a tinge of condescension.

Laura nodded.

"Tell me, what was he like as a teacher? I'll bet you thought he was fascinating," Sheila prodded.

Michael studied Laura's reaction. She shrugged and looked noncommittal. "I guess some people thought he was fascinating."

Michael laughed. "If you want to hear something positive about me, Sheila, you're asking the wrong person. Laura was definitely not one of my fans."

Laura shot him a scathing look and snapped, "If I recall correctly, I wasn't your favorite student, either."

"Ease up, Laura," Bobby said.

"Sorry," Laura snapped.

"My fault," Michael replied. He was disappointed to have this dialogue with Laura end, even if it had been just an argument.

The discussion turned to school sports. Michael suggested that Bobby should round up a few friends to play a game of basketball or maybe volleyball in the school gymnasium.

"Great! Tomorrow night?" Bobby gave an exuberant grin.

Bobby really was likeable. No wonder Laura loved him. "No problem," Michael said. "Tomorrow's fine. Just give me a call and I'll open the school."

Laura sat quietly listening to the conversation between Michael and Bobby. Michael and Sheila finished their meal by the time Laura's and Bobby's plates arrived.

Sheila picked up her purse and stood up. "We should leave, Michael," she said.

Michael was surprised at her reaction. He had ignored her a little, but he had never known her to be so impatient. Laura and Bobby had obviously ruined her evening.

"All right," he said. "Let's get moving." He turned back to Laura and Bobby. "It was nice seeing you. Don't forget to give me a call, Bobby."

While waiting at the cashier's desk for his bill to be rung up, Michael looked back at Laura. When he noticed that Laura had been watching him, he felt a ray of hope.

He caught her eye. She colored and immediately turned her attention to the food on her plate.

The movie was billed as a very funny slapstick comedy but Laura's mind was elsewhere.

"That was great, wasn't it," Bobby said as they walked out of the theater.

Laura smiled in agreement. She hoped he wouldn't ask her any questions because she didn't know what the movie had been about. Her emotions had been in turmoil the entire evening, what with Bobby wanting her and then Michael wanting somebody else.

Michael's date had definitely been beautiful and sophisticated. If only she had taken the time to dress up. But it wouldn't have mattered anyway, Laura thought. She still wouldn't have stood a chance next to the beautiful Sheila.

It was close to midnight and Laura was tired. All she wanted was to get home and go to bed.

"I haven't laughed so hard in a long time. How about you?" Bobby was in good spirits.

Laura smiled and nodded in agreement. Laughed? She had felt like crying, but Bobby didn't seem to notice.

"Let's go for a hamburger," he suggested.

"Eat again? Let's not."

"You never used to turn down food," he said. "How about we just go for a cup of coffee."

"Not tonight, Bobby. I'm not hungry and I'm really beat. Let's go straight home, okay?"

"If you say so," he grumbled.

Laura yawned. She slouched down in the seat of Bobby's truck and leaned her head back against the headrest. She was tired. It hadn't been smart to stay out so late midweek. She had too much to do. She mentally made a list of the things she would work on in the morning.

"What did you think of the coach's girlfriend? Pretty good-looking, wouldn't you say?" Bobby asked.

"She was okay."

"It's nice of him to let us use the gym, don't you think? He said we could even make it a regular thing if we want. Maybe once a week all winter long," he continued.

"Is that what he said?"

"Didn't you hear him? It'll be great. I'm going to phone the guys first thing in the morning. You want to help me make some phone calls?"

"I don't think so, Bobby. I'm going to be awfully busy."

Bobby shrugged. "Okay. I'll do the calling myself."

They rode on in silence for a while. Bobby turned

on the radio and played with the dial until the strains of a plaintive country and western song filled the vehicle.

Then he draped his right arm on the back of the seat and let his fingers caress Laura's cheek. "It's good to have you back home, Laura," he said. She closed her eyes and imagined what it would be like if the hand belonged to Michael.

"You don't know how much I missed you," Bobby continued.

The song was sad. Laura swallowed the lump in her throat.

"I know you don't want to talk about it yet, but we'll have to talk soon."

"No, Bobby."

"Just listen, okay?" he said. "Mom and Dad are going to be retiring and moving into town, and I'm going to take over running the farm. I'd like you there with me."

What was the use of disagreeing? Maybe she should settle for Bobby. She would never stand a chance with Michael anyway.

"With your mom so sick, your dad's been talking about moving into Lethbridge. Then your mom can be closer to the hospital."

"That would make it a lot easier for them both."

"I told your dad I could farm his place too." Bobby explained his plans to her. "I talked to them about us getting married. They thought it was a good idea."

They all had plans for her life—all the people who loved her. But didn't any of them care how she felt?

"No."

"Why not? They say it's okay with them."

"No, Bobby." Why wasn't he listening to her?

"You could choose where you want us to live. We could stay at either place."

She looked out her window at the starry sky. It had to be love. She wouldn't settle for less.

"You're a great guy, Bobby, and I wish with all my heart that I could marry you," she said. She could sense that this time he was listening. She hoped that he was finally understanding what she had been trying to tell him all along.

"You're not going to give me a definite no," he said.

She sat up and looked at him. "I don't want to hurt you, but please believe me when I say that I can't marry you."

"There someone else, isn't there?" he said. "Someone's waiting for you in Calgary."

She could feel the tears stinging her cheeks, and she looked out the window so he wouldn't notice. "No, there's no one waiting for me."

"Well then, darn it, Laura, you're just being obstinate," he said. He stepped down hard on the gas pedal and the truck roared down the highway.

"Take it easy, Bobby."

He slowed down a little. "Okay, but I'm not giving up," he said. "I love you, Laura, and I'm going to make you love me."

Chapter Ten

Laura pushed the scrambled eggs around on her plate. She didn't feel hungry today.

She thought about the future and it didn't look so great. Love. She'd just have to do without it. But without Michael, what did she have to look forward to? Just a nice, comfortable, boring existence.

Her father sat across the table from her, caught up in his own thoughts. She suspected that he and her mother knew Bobby was going to propose to her last night. As a matter of fact, she was pretty sure that her parents had a hand in making it happen. But what was the use of getting upset with them?

"More coffee, Dad?" she asked.

He nodded. "I'll take another cup."

She took both their cups to where the coffee pot was plugged in, set the cups on the counter, refilled them, and returned them to the table without comment.

"You're not saying much," her father said as he

took his cup. "Something's just got to be the matter. You're usually talking a mile a minute."

She shook her head. "No, nothing's the matter." She moved the sugar bowl closer to him.

"Are you sick?" He put three teaspoons of sugar into his coffee and reached for the cream. "You're not coming down with something, are you?"

"I'm fine," she said, handing him the pitcher. "I guess I shouldn't have stayed out so late last night."

He topped his cup with the cream, gave it a quick stir, and took a big gulp. "Well, something must have happened. Did you and Bobby have a fight?"

"No, Dad. Nothing happened and nothing's wrong, really. I'm just tired, that's all."

"We're all tired." He went back to stirring. "I don't know what I'm going to do," he said. He studied the coffee as it swirled around in his cup. "I'm afraid, Laura. I don't think your mother's getting any better."

"You can't think that, Dad. The doctors are doing all they can. She'll get better."

Her father shook his head. "We can hope and we can pray and we can pretend all we like, but the reality is that the cancer's back and it's probably spreading. All that radiation and all the chemotherapy didn't do a darn thing for her, except make her feel sicker."

Laura had never seen her father so down. He had always been the strong one, always hopeful. It hurt to see him this way. "We just have to keep hoping."

"You're right there," he said. "We've got to keep hoping and making sure your mother doesn't lose hope." He took another big gulp of coffee and wiped his mouth with the back of his hand. "Let's talk about you now."

"What have I done now?"

"It's what you're not doing. Maybe it's none of my business, but you know that your mother's got her heart set on seeing you settled. What's wrong with setting her mind at ease? You and Bobby have been going together since you were kids, and from what he tells us, he wants to marry you. What's stopping you, Laura? Bobby's a good man."

"Please, Dad. Don't you start on me too."

"You could do a heck of a lot worse than marrying Bobby."

She could feel the tears blurring her vision. "I thought you would be on my side."

"I am on your side. How old are you now, twenty-seven, twenty-eight? Why do you want to teach other people's kids? You should be thinking of having some of your own. You can teach them. I'm telling you, Laura, you should grab a good thing when you got the chance."

"It's my life, Dad. I don't want to talk about it any more." She got up from the table and added what was left of her breakfast to Shep's dish.

"Okay, I won't say another word." Her father's voice was sad and tired. "Except, don't you go turning him down just to be stubborn. There's no time to be stubborn."

"I know that."

"Your mother's got to go into the hospital for more tests tomorrow, and I've got to finish that field. Can you drive her in this time."

Laura turned back to face him. "Of course I'll take her, Dad. What time does she have to be there?"

"It's on the calendar." He pointed to the calendar on the wall by the telephone. "I think she's supposed to check in at nine and stay there all day."

"Don't worry—I'll get her there."

"She'll like that. She's missed you these past few years. I know she nags at you sometimes, but that's because she loves you. She wants to see you happy."

"I know she loves me, but if she wants to see me happy, she's going about it all wrong." Laura resented her parents' intrusion into her life, and at the same time she felt ashamed that she couldn't be less selfish. "I love her too, Dad, but I can't marry someone just to please her." Her throat felt tight. She had always wanted to please her parents, but this was different. "You can't want me to marry Bobby just because that's what Mom wants. That's asking too much, Dad."

Mr. Hart patted her hand. "Do what you think is right. Just be careful you don't turn down a good man out of rebellion." Laura shook her head, but her father went on, "I've seen that rebellious streak of yours before."

"I know you have. But not this time. Honest, Dad, Bobby and I are just friends. I know he's a good guy, and maybe I should love him, but I don't. You wouldn't want me to marry somebody I don't love, would you?"

"I guess not," her father said. "Not if you're sure you don't love him."

The telephone rang. Laura got up from the table and went to answer it. It was Bobby, telling her that he had called several friends and that the volleyball game had been arranged. They were all going to meet at the school after supper.

"That sounds great," she said. "Have a good time."

"You have to come, too. Some of the girls are going to be out there. You'll have a good time."

"I don't know," Laura hesitated. Going out with Bobby last night had been a mistake. If she went out with him tonight, he would probably consider it encouragement.

"Come on, you don't want them to think you're stuck up," Bobby insisted.

She could think of a million excuses for staying home but when it came right down to it, there wasn't any good reason. In the end, she agreed to go. After all, it would be a good opportunity to see some of the old gang. "Okay," she said. "But don't get any ideas."

"Who me?" Bobby played the innocent.

It didn't sound good. Maybe she shouldn't go.

She had just finished talking to Bobby when the telephone rang again. It was Michael. Her heart skipped a beat. Michael called! He looked up her telephone number and dialed it!

". . . have arrived," he said.

She came out of her trance to realize that she had been so excited that she hadn't heard what he said. "What was that? I'm sorry, I didn't hear," she said. "It must be a poor connection."

His voice came back strong and clear. The only connection that wasn't working was the one between her head and her heart. "The textbooks for your students have arrived," he told her. "Would you like to come to the school and help me unpack them? You can check to see that everything's here."

Laura's heart sank. That was all he wanted, for her to come to school and do more work. Her blood began to boil. Darn it, she wasn't his slave. She wasn't getting paid for all these extra days she was spending at the school. She didn't mind doing the work, but he had his nerve, demanding that she do extra work.

"Not today," she said. "I'm too busy."

There was a long pause on the line and then he asked, "Will you be coming to the school this evening?"

"I don't know," she said. "I might be. Bobby just finished twisting my arm to convince me to come."

"I hope to see you there," he said. Laura thought he sounded subdued.

Michael switched the lights on in the gymnasium. This was his favorite place. When it was empty like this, it gave him a feeling of anticipation, of waiting for something to happen, expecting the excitement to begin. During practices, the general feeling was camaraderie and physical exhilaration, and during the games, there was tension, anticipation, excitement and exhilaration. Tonight was everything combined.

Soon the players would be arriving. It would be nice to see his old students. In some respects tonight was almost a mini-reunion of some of the students from the first class he ever taught. Laura would be here.

He unlocked the front door of the school and went back to his office to wait for them to arrive.

Michael sat in his swivel chair looking out the window. Not a cloud in the sky, and the sun was getting low on the horizon. Another half hour or so before it went down. It would be a beautiful sunset. What was he doing sitting inside when he should be out there watching the light show?

Bobby's half-ton pulled into the parking lot. Bobby got out and started toward the school. Wasn't Laura with him? Then Bobby stopped, looked back, and waited. The passenger door opened and Laura climbed out.

A minute later, two cars and another truck arrived.

Bobby and Laura waited in the parking lot for their friends to get out.

There were shouts and laughter, a confusion of chatter, and squeals and giggles of obvious delight. Michael watched the interaction among the old friends, happy that he had suggested the get-together. Laura was in good spirits. She hugged them all and chattered like a chipmunk. It was nice to see her that way. If only she had been even half as delighted to see him.

The noisy group entered the school. Michael listened to their banter as they moved down the hall toward the gymnasium. They knew where to find the equipment, and they knew how to set it up, so he took his time joining them. Let them enjoy rediscovering their school.

By the time Michael got to the gym, Bobby and Frank had already changed and were taking the volleyball standards and nets out of the equipment room. "Hi, guys," he called out.

Bobby waved. "Hey, coach!"

"Bobby, Frank," Michael said. "I see you're just about set up. Did you find everything you need?"

"Yup, everything's here," said Bobby.

Frank ran over to shake Michael's hand. "Good to see you again, Mr. Foster."

"You too, Frank. How are you doing?"

Just then, Don, Pete and Jake came out of the changing room and gathered around Michael just like the old days.

"Coach Foster, my man. How are you doing?" Don held out the palms of his hands.

"Hey, Don." Michael slapped down on Don's hands in the traditional greeting.

"We hear you're the boss now," Peter said. "All right, Mr. Foster!"

Michael laughed. "Thanks, Pete."

Jake was still the shy, polite one. "We really appreciate you letting us play, Mr. Foster," he said.

"We'll have to do it again," Michael replied.

The girls came out of their dressing room in a tight cluster, just the way they always had. There were four of them: Laura, Mary, Susan, and a girl Michael didn't recognize.

"Hi, ladies, all set to play?" he asked.

Susan greeted him with a giggle, "Hi, Mr. Foster."

Mary said, "We sure are," and Laura just nodded in reply. It turned out that the other girl was Jake's girlfriend, a girl from the next town.

"Is this all of you, or are there more coming?" he asked.

"I think this is it," Bobby replied. "It was kind of short notice for some of the others."

"Okay, have a good time." Michael headed out of the gym. He didn't want to stifle their conversation.

"Hey, coach, don't go," Bobby called out. "You have to stay and play with us."

"Yeah, we need an extra player," Frank added.

Michael loved to play, so it didn't take much encouragement for him to agree. "Okay, I'll just go and lock the front door."

When he came back the teams had been selected. Five players on each side: Jake, his girlfriend, Bobby, Laura, and Frank on one side of the net; Pete, Don, Susan, Mary, and himself on the other.

The evening progressed with a great deal of happy noise and much kidding, teasing, and joking. There were many comments, jokes, and stories of past glories, but all Michael could think about was Laura on the other side of the net.

The unpleasant part of the evening for Michael was watching the familiar way Bobby behaved around Laura.

Every time she hit the ball, he reacted by saying, "That's my girl!" or "Way to go, Laura!" and each time he took the opportunity to touch her. He either put his arm around her, or stroked her arm, or patted her back. Michael hated it.

Laura, on the other hand, seemed to be too wrapped up in her own thoughts to discourage him. She didn't even seem to notice.

At the end of the evening, after the equipment had been put away and everyone had showered, Don said, "It's too soon to go home. Why don't we go for pizza?"

"Yeah, why not," said Bobby.

Jake turned to his girlfriend. "What do you think? Would you like to go?"

"Sure," she said.

"I'm in," said Mary.

"Yeah," Frank said. "How about you, coach?"

Michael's nerves were taut. There was no way that he would be able to sit and quietly eat his pizza while Bobby made out with Laura. "No, not me. You kids go and have a good time," Michael replied. "Count me out."

"Aw, come on, coach," Bobby said.

Michael shook his head. "Thanks. Some other time."

"I don't want to go to out tonight either," Laura said to Bobby. "I'd like to go home," she said.

"Gee, Laura. Don't be that way." Bobby was obviously disappointed.

"I'm sorry, Bobby. I just don't want to go."

Michael felt a sting of satisfaction. It served Bobby right for being so familiar with Laura.

"We won't stay out late." Bobby tried to talk her into staying. "A couple of slices of pizza, and then I'll take you home."

"No, Bobby, and quit trying to push me into doing what you want," Laura snapped. "I have to get up early tomorrow."

"I can drive her home if you want, Bobby," Michael offered.

Bobby hesitated.

"I don't feel like pizza tonight," Michael continued. He wanted to be with her, but he was afraid to seem too eager. He watched the play of emotions on her face.

She seemed happy at the offer but then she looked him in the eye and said, "I don't want to put you out."

She hadn't said no. His heart was pounding but he tried to look casual. "It's no trouble."

For a moment Bobby looked as though he might change his mind about going with the group, but then someone called out, "Are you coming, Bobby?"

"Yeah," he called back. He turned to Laura. "If you have to go home, I guess it's okay if the coach takes you."

Michael's pulse was racing. He couldn't believe his luck. Quite by accident, he was going to be alone with Laura.

"Just let me lock up and then we can leave," he said to her.

Bobby slapped him on the shoulder. "Thanks for driving Laura home, coach. I appreciate it."

"Don't mention it," Michael replied, too happy to feel guilty.

Chapter Eleven

Eleven o'clock. Laura sat on the bench beside the school's entrance waiting for Michael to switch off the lights and lock up the building. It was a warm and peaceful summer evening. She could smell the sweet, ripe aroma of alfalfa hay wafting in from the field across the street. The scent was much stronger and headier at night. But then, everything seemed magnified at night.

Providence School sprawled on the edge of town, bordered on three sides by farmland. Houses encroached only as far as Sixth Street, a graveled road that ran on one side the schoolyard. There were no street lights. The only street lights in Providence were the ones on Main Street. Even the windows of the houses were dark. It was unlikely that all the residents had gone away. They were probably in bed. The town of Providence seemed asleep.

She could hear the drone of a vehicle a few blocks

away. It was probably Bobby's truck, or maybe
Frank's, heading for the highway. The Pizza Palace
was thirty miles away, in the next town. By the time
they got there, placed their order, and waited for the
pizza to be baked, it would be close to midnight. If
she'd gone with them, she would not be back home
much before two.

That was not what she wanted. She didn't want to
sit in a noisy young people's hangout when she could
be out here, looking at the moon and smelling the
freshly mown hay.

"It's a beautiful evening, isn't it?"

She turned to look behind her. Michael was standing on the top step, leaning on the railing. She wondered how long he had been there.

"How do you do that?" she asked.

"Do what?"

"Sneak around like that?"

He laughed. "You were a million miles away. I
could have been playing the bagpipes and you
wouldn't have heard me." He had a good laugh—
happy and infectious.

She grinned up at him. "Please not the bagpipes.
Just stamp your feet a little or maybe cough next
time."

He took a deep breath of the scented air. "I love the
smell of freshly mown hay, even if it does mean the
end of summer."

It was as though he had been reading her mind. "Me
too."

"Peaceful, isn't it?" he said.

"Yeah." Laura sat down again and leaned back to
look at the sky. "I can't believe there are so many
stars. The whole time I was in Calgary, I never saw

such a blue sky and so many stars. I'd forgotten just how many stars one could see out here away from city lights."

He came down the steps and sat beside her on the bench. "That's one of the things that's keeping me here," he said, "the evenings." He seemed almost too near but there was no way she could move away from him without making him aware of her discomfiture.

"When I look up at the sky, I feel very small and the universe seems endless," she said. "I can't help but dream."

"There's nothing wrong with dreaming," he said. "On a night like tonight, anything seems possible."

"And my problems seem so petty."

"If you think they're problems, then to you they're not petty," he said.

"In the scale of things, they're pretty minor."

"Do you want to talk?" he asked. "I'll listen. If ever you need somebody to talk to, Laura, I want you to feel you can come to me."

She looked up at him and saw genuine concern for her in his eyes. But tell him her problems? He had to be joking.

"Anytime," he added. "I'm here for you."

She had a feeling he meant it, but that didn't help. Her biggest problems were ones she couldn't discuss with him. How could she tell him that he was her problem? Or that she was in love? And if she did, what advice would he give her?

He picked up her sports bag. "Come on, let's get you home."

Aside from his vehicle, the lot was empty. Laura was very aware of being alone with him, and that in a short while the two of them would be alone in a very confined space. As she waited for him to unlock the passenger door, she could hear the loud rhythm of her heartbeat. She wondered if Michael could hear it, wondered if he sensed her nervousness, her breathless anticipation.

He opened the door. She climbed in. He closed it, went around to the driver's side, and got in.

She held her breath. He was silent and she wanted him to say something.

"Buckle up," he said, doing up his own seat belt.

She relaxed. He started the van.

"It's funny, you driving a van," she said.

"Why's that?"

"Well, somehow I expected you to drive something different."

"What did you expect, a beat-up wreck?" He turned the key and started the motor.

He should be on a white horse. "Oh, I don't know," she said. "A Jeep or a truck."

"I wouldn't mind," he said. "I guess most of the guys around here drive trucks. They need to haul stuff for their farms. For me, a van was more practical. I was doing so much coaching that I decided to buy one. It seemed the ideal vehicle for transporting my team," he said. "I took the players with me. That way I could keep an eye on them and we never had to worry about transportation."

"You used to take the team on the school bus."

"Yeah, but the van is smaller, just big enough for the team."

"I thought you liked having the cheerleaders along," she teased. "Did you find them too distracting?"

"You were a brat, Laura. You were hard to figure

out. You still are. I can't decide if the red sports car is or isn't you."

"What do you mean?" Laura sat tensely, waiting for his response.

He seemed thoughtful as he put the van into reverse and backed out of the parking space. "I don't know what I mean," he said. "When it comes to you, I never know what I mean." He switched gears and drove out of the lot.

Michael drove out of the town in silence and maintained the silence for the first half mile or so. Moonlight gave the countryside a soft silver sheen that was almost magical. The road was a beam ahead of them. They were all alone in the stillness and Laura found herself surprisingly calm. So many times she had dreamed of being with him, and here she was, in the warm cocoon of the vehicle, feeling whole and significant.

Michael leaned toward her as he reached for the radio dial. Laura shivered at his nearness and leaned away. She needed to keep a space between them. He was like a magnet. She knew that if he got too close, his magnetic field would pull her in.

The radio voice of Willie Nelson sang and Laura felt goose bumps rise. She looked at Michael. He was looking at her. The words of the song hung in the air.

She needed to break the silence, to block out the voice. "It was good to see everybody again," she said. "It's been a long time since we were all together."

Michael nodded. "You were quite the group, always ready for a good time."

"We sure did have some good times. This time of year, most evenings, we used to go out to the canal. The water would be nice and warm, great for swimming. We'd park the cars on the bank so the headlights lit the water and dive off the bridge into the deep water up above the dam," she said.

"That was dangerous."

"Yeah, I guess it was but we never gave it any thought. Have you ever been there?"

"Just once, right after the accident. Mr. Walsh took me out to have a look at the famous swimming hole."

"What accident?" She remembered a few close calls—kids who weren't very strong swimmers getting caught in the current. But each time they had managed to grab the rope and pull themselves to shore. That didn't stop them from going back. As teenagers, they believed that nothing drastic would ever happen to them. They were immortal.

"It was three years ago," he said. "A boy drowned in that canal. You never heard about it?"

"No, I hadn't heard. Who was it?"

"Barry Mason."

"Was he from here? I don't remember anyone by that name."

"They were new. Had only been here about a year, bought a place west of town, out near the dogleg turn-off."

"I think I know the place you mean. It used to be pretty run-down, and it had a house that was only partly above ground."

"That's right. They've fixed it up considerably. Barry was the oldest child, in grade seven, just thirteen."

"That's terrible. How did it happen?"

"It was around the middle of May. Barry and a couple of his friends skipped school that afternoon and rode their bikes to the canal. There had been a lot of rain and runoff, so the canal was pretty full and the water was moving pretty fast. The boys said Barry got caught in the undertow, went over the drop, and didn't come up. One of the boys went in after Barry and he almost didn't make it back to shore."

"How did the boys cope?"

"They had a tough time of it. It was pretty scary for them, plus they were feeling pretty guilty about being there in the first place, but it's been a while."

"There used to be a safety rope stretched across the canal."

"I don't think there was one—too early in the season. In any case, the accident was what pushed the town into deciding to build a swimming pool."

"So now Providence has a swimming pool?"

He nodded. "It's the big yellow structure right next to the civic center. It just opened this summer. The younger children like it, but unfortunately, I think the older kids still prefer to hang around the canal."

"It's because it's dangerous and because there are no adults around," she said. "At least, that was the thrill when I was young. There was a nice safe spot down past the waterfall, but that was too tame. We never went there."

As they drove past the Berent farm, Michael said, "This is where Bobby lives, isn't it?"

"That's right. Just another half mile and I'm home," Laura said, trying to keep the disappointment out of her voice.

"That's pretty handy, you living just down the road from Bobby. Rumor has it that you have come home to marry him."

Laura studied Michael. His eyes were on the road

and his jaw seemed clenched tight. Why was he asking? "No, I'm not going to marry Bobby."

"Why not?" he insisted, still not looking at her. "Bobby's a good man, and there's obviously something between you."

She wanted him to look at her. "Bobby's been my best friend for as long as I can remember and I like him very much, but not the way you mean. Not enough to get married."

"I'm surprised to hear that. You dated in high school and you're still dating ten years later. Don't tell me there's nothing going on between you, that he never made a pass at you?"

"Bobby doesn't make passes," she snapped.

"Well, what was he doing tonight? He had his hands all over you," he said. "Not that you seemed to mind."

"He did not!" she snapped back. "He slapped me on the back. What's wrong with that? You guys are always slapping each other on the back."

"It didn't look the same."

"Well it was. He was congratulating me on a good hit. He didn't have any ulterior motives. Anyway, what's it to you?"

"Okay, I'm sorry." Now Michael did look at her, and she found it disconcerting.

"It's just that Bobby's not like that. He's always been honest and straightforward. He says what he means. That's what I like best about him."

"You like people to be honest," he said. "Somehow that doesn't surprise me. You want me to be honest with you, right? But will you be honest with me?"

"Of course."

"Okay then, tell the truth," he said. "Why is it that

you always give me such a hard time? What is it that I do to make you dislike me so much?"

"Dislike you? Look who's talking!" Laura exploded. "You're the one who dislikes me. You always did."

"Don't be ridiculous."

"It's true."

"What have I ever done to make you think that?"

"All kinds of things. You were always on my case, always telling me my work wasn't good enough."

"It wasn't good enough," he agreed. "I wanted you to do better."

"And then, remember graduation night? You danced with all the girls, except me." Laura bit her lip and wished she hadn't mentioned that night.

"Graduation night?" Michael seemed surprised. "I did ask you to dance. It was you who didn't want to dance with me."

"Well, why should I have? I was the last one you asked. And even then, the only reason you asked me was because there wasn't anyone else left for you to ask."

They drove into the yard and were greeted by Shep's loud barking. Michael killed the engine and switched off the lights. "That's not the way I remember that night," Michael said.

"Well, that's the way it was," Laura said. She rolled down her window and greeted the dog, "Quiet, Shep. It's just me."

Shep stopped barking, wagged his tail, and returned to his bed under the front step.

"Shall we just talk for a while, Laura?"

"What's there to talk about?"

Michael heard the hurt in her voice and the memory of that evening became vivid.

"I wasn't rejecting you, Laura. If it seemed that way, I'm sorry, but think back, Laura. You weren't lacking for dance partners that night. Every time I looked, you were out there on that dance floor having a great time," he said. "You didn't come by to say hello. The other students did, but not you. The way I saw it, you couldn't be bothered."

"I was going to, but you were always busy with other people, talking or dancing," she said. "I was the very last one you danced with."

"You were busy carrying on with Bobby. I didn't want to interrupt."

Laura's hands were clenched in her lap. "I was trying to have a good time," she said as she studied her knuckles.

He felt that he should let the topic go, but he couldn't. "You obviously didn't have a good time when you finally did dance with me. You ran off."

Her voice was almost inaudible and she didn't look up. "I couldn't dance with you," she said. "That's why I left. I ran to the bathroom, and then I was too embarrassed to come out."

She had been embarrassed?

He had been shattered.

He remembered looking around, hoping the scene had gone unnoticed, but then he caught the principal's eye and knew the older man had seen it all.

They sat in silence for a time. Then Laura said, "I wanted so much to impress you, to gain your approval, but all I ever did was make things worse. I was miserable."

"I'm sorry, Laura. Let's leave the misunderstandings behind," Michael said. "Let's start over."

"Mmm," she said. The lump in her throat made it difficult for her to reply.

Michael's arm was around her shoulders. "Laura . . ."

"I'd better go," she said, but she didn't make a move.

He gently pulled her in toward him.

She rested her head on his shoulder. "I should invite you in for coffee but I don't want to wake up my mom and dad."

Michael felt the silky softness of her hair against his cheek, smelled the fragrance of peach shampoo. He didn't need coffee. "It's a beautiful evening. I don't want it to end."

"Neither do I," she said as she snuggled up against his chest. Her breath tickled his throat.

"Do you want to go for a drive?" His heart was afraid she'd say no—his head hoped she would.

"Okay." Her voice was a murmur against his throat.

He started the van.

Chapter Twelve

The van followed the beacon of its own light beam. Laura sat in silence, watching the road and anticipating . . . what?

The radio was playing love songs. It was a conspiracy—the moon, the stars, the love songs. They were all on her side.

Michael had been quiet since they left her place. He drove, eyes straight ahead, concentrating on the road. Laura watched his reflection in the windshield and wondered what he was thinking. Was he regretting the decision, or was this evening magical for him too? Did he hope, as she did, that the magic wouldn't end?

But maybe it was a mistake.

What on earth was the matter with her? This was what she wanted, had wanted, had dreamed about—to be alone with Michael, to have him hold her in his arms and kiss her and kiss her and kiss her. She wanted it and she was afraid.

Out her side window, she could see the harvest moon, a big crystal ball. What could it tell her?

What would he want? What if . . . ? She felt breathless at the thought. With him, she was an inexperienced child. What if the bubble burst?

She tried to sound casual, as though this was just another ride. "Where are we going?" she asked. She noticed that her voice sounded breathless. Breathless was sexy when Marilyn Monroe talked that way. She kept it breathless. "You never said where you were taking me."

He looked at her and smiled. "There's a special place I want to show you," he said.

A special place? He was taking her to a special place. She felt the hair on the back of her neck prickle. A special place.

They were silent through Huey Lewis' rendition of "The Power of Love" and Diana Ross singing "Endless Love".

"Is it much farther?" Laura asked.

She was intensely aware that their conversation was in slow motion, like a couple of actors who had to prepare their lines before saying them.

"We're almost there."

They drove another five or ten minutes. It was hard to tell—time had become irrelevant. Then they turned into a driveway and followed it into a grove of trees.

She recognized the place—the old Martin place. It had been off limits when she was young. Everyone knew that Mr. Martin was strange and dangerous, and that he wouldn't think twice about using his shotgun to chase away intruders. That was what had made it so tempting for Bobby, Frank, herself and the rest of the teenagers. Outsmarting "Old Man Martin" and stealing crabapples off the big old tree at the end of his lane was a real challenge and turned into quite an adventure.

Laura was in ninth grade the first time she and her friends had a run-in with Old Man Martin. Frank had just gotten his driver's license and took a few friends for a spin in his mother's Caddy. The drive took them past the Martin place.

Laura had been the first one to see the big old apple tree laden with fruit. "Look at that tree. Those apples sure look good," was all she had said. But one comment led to another, and finally, ignoring the large KEEP OUT sign, they had all climbed over the fence and gone after the apples.

Frank had started to climb it when the dogs came, and right behind the dogs, a furious Old Man Martin, waving his shotgun and shouting threats. That was the most terrifying run of Laura's life. Somehow, she got past the barbed wire fence without ripping her clothes and into the car before the dogs got there. They had gotten away, and luckily no one had been hurt.

Later in the fall, they had returned to the Martin place to play a Halloween prank. The hermit lived in a primitive old cabin with no indoor plumbing. His was the last of the old outdoor toilets in the area, and it begged to be tipped. This time, they had come prepared. They dressed in dark clothes, drove with the lights off to avoid detection, and brought meat for the dogs.

Everything had gone more or less as planned, but Mr. Martin, hearing some noise, had come out to investigate. When he saw his toilet tipped over, he hadn't thought it was very funny, and neither had they when he started shooting in their direction.

Laura never did tell her parents about it. They would have been very upset with her and angry with Bobby.

"This is the Martin place," she said. "We're not allowed to trespass."

Michael pulled the van to a stop right in the middle of the driveway. "Mr. Martin is not here anymore. The poor old fellow's been in a nursing home for almost a year now."

"I know. Bobby told me the place was for sale." At the mention of Bobby, Michael's smile disappeared. Laura felt a small thrill at the thought that Michael might be jealous.

"It's been sold," he said. "Way back in the spring. I'm surprised Bobby didn't know."

"He said it was so run-down that he didn't think anybody would buy it, but it doesn't look so bad to me," she said.

"It's had a lot of work done to it."

"I'm surprised you found it. Nobody's been allowed on this property for years."

"The first time I came here, it was with Mr. Walsh. He brought me here to fish in the river. That was a few years ago. After that, I came quite often."

"What about Mr. Martin? Didn't he chase you away?"

"No. Why would he do that?"

"Well . . . he was crazy. Everybody said so."

"He was lonely and old and tired—I don't know if he was crazy or not. Maybe he was. Mr. Walsh felt sorry for him, out here all by himself, and so did I. Poor old man, living in a pile of garbage."

"Are you sure it's okay for us to be here?"

"Yes, I'm sure." He switched off the engine and

then the headlights. "Come on. You have to see this," he said.

"I don't know. Maybe we shouldn't."

"It's safe," he said. "The path is good. The moon is so bright it's almost like daylight, and there's a nice little spot on the riverbank for us to sit and enjoy the evening."

She opened her door. She didn't want him opening it for her, didn't want him to come too near, but he was around to her side just as she was stepping down.

He reached for her hand. At his touch, Laura's breath sucked in sharply, and she recoiled as if from a hot stove.

Michael took her hand and held it. Her pulse was racing wildly. She wanted to run, to escape before he discovered how she felt. She was very conscious of her fingers in the palm of his hand. All the nerve ends tingled.

Now what? She waited for his next move. When he released her and turned back to the vehicle, she felt a sick hollow of disappointment in her stomach.

"It is a really nice spot, but there aren't any benches out there," he said. "I'll take a blanket for us to sit on." He slid opened the side door, took the plaid blanket that was draped over the back seat, and slung it over his shoulder. "Come on."

He held out his hand and she took it. Disappointment turned to nervous anticipation as he led her down the path.

And there was the river. Moonlight had turned the scene all soft and magical. Weeping willows skirted the clearing, their silver leaves cascading and glistening in the moonlight. Silver ripples whispered in the silver stream.

"Beautiful!" she whispered, and even the whisper seemed intrusive in this magical place.

They stood in silence, side by side, not quite touching, and she shivered at his nearness.

"Cold?" he asked, putting an arm around her shoulders.

She leaned into his strength. "No."

"Laura . . ."

She looked up and his eyes smoldered into hers. Her heart thumped and she could hardly breathe. She knew that she should look away, should move away, but she couldn't.

She wasn't sure how it happened. She hadn't moved and neither had he, but they were drawing together as if by some enormous magnet. Closer and closer.

She felt his hand outlining her cheek, her chin, her lips, and then slowly caressing its way past her ear to the back of her neck, and then he kissed her—a sweet touch, a tender question.

She had dreamed of this, had waited years for it and yet when it happened it was unlike anything she had imagined. An explosion of sensations shook her body. Her knees went weak and she clung to him.

His lips caressed her face, and he held her to him. His breathing was rough and his heart was hammering.

Michael wanted her. She was everything he had ever dreamed and more. The warmth of her breath, the soft heat of her lips—he couldn't get enough of her. He yearned to drink her in; his very being wanted to draw her in.

Her response to his kisses left no doubt that she wanted him too. He stroked her back, pulling her in even closer. She was so soft, so vulnerable.

This was wrong. This was not why he brought her here.

Wasn't it?

Reluctantly, he pulled his lips away and held her to him. He could sense her vulnerability, and every fiber of his being yearned for her.

"Laura," he whispered in her hair, and then he moved her away from him so that he could look at her. "I want you more than anything," he said. "But not like this."

"Why not, Michael?" she said, her eyes big and luminous.

He stroked her cheek. "Laura, my sweet fiery Laura. You set me on fire. It's all I can do to keep from burning us."

She held his hand to her cheek, then turned her face and kissed his palm. "I've never felt like this about anyone but you."

"I want it to be true, but I don't want to take the chance that it's the moonlight and the magic of this place that is winning you. I want it to be me."

"I love you, Michael. It's not the moonlight." She snuggled in against his chest. "I know I'll feel the same way in the morning, and I'll feel the same way at noon."

It took all his will power. He took her wrists and moved her away from him. "Well then, we can wait, can't we? I want you to be sure. I don't want you to have regrets," he said.

She made a face at him. "I don't believe it, you're an old fuddy-duddy," she teased.

"Maybe so. How about we get together tomorrow? See how you feel then."

"I can't." There was disappointment in her voice.

"I'll be going into town tomorrow. I'll be there all day."

"Me too. I have to run some errands and pick up a few supplies. Maybe we could meet for lunch—that is, if you can get away from whatever you are doing long enough to eat."

"It's my mom. I'm taking her to the hospital for some tests. She has to be at the cancer clinic for most of the day."

"I heard your mother had been sick. Cancer?"

Laura nodded. "Yes. It's been a tough road for her."

"I'm so sorry to hear that, Laura."

"She's had surgery, radiation, chemo, the works."

"And now? How does she seem?"

"I don't know. I don't want to even speculate if she's okay. She doesn't say much, but I can tell that she's worried and that scares me."

"Sometime the worry can be the worst part."

Laura shrugged. "It's hard not to worry. I guess these tests will tell us something."

"So you will be staying with her all day tomorrow."

"No, I'll have time to join you for lunch."

"Okay, then. Noon tomorrow. Is the Garden Grill okay?"

"Garden Grill at high noon? Sure."

"Come on, there's a fire pit down by the river. How about I light a fire and we can sit and talk a while. You probably don't believe me, but that was my original intention."

Michael set the blanket down for Laura to sit and went to light the fire. Laura noticed that there was a stack of firewood and some kindling ready for use beside the pit. "Someone went to a lot of trouble chopping firewood," she said. "It doesn't seem right for us to use it."

"It was me. I come out here a lot, and I like sitting by the fire." He built a teepee out of kindling, put a crumpled up newspaper page in the middle and added a couple of pieces of split log. "It reminds me of my Scout years. That's where I got my love of the outdoors, and that's where I learned how to start a proper campfire," he said as he set a match to the paper. The fire instantly took. Flames licked the kindling, and soon the logs were burning.

"You learned well," Laura said.

They sat side by side on the blanket leaning back against the riverbank, their feet warmed by the fire.

It was so peaceful. Michael's arm held her, and she leaned her head on his shoulder. "This is such a beautiful evening. I'll never forget it," Laura said.

"That makes two of us."

"And this place! I love it. I'd love to come out here with my sketchbook and my paints."

"I remember you were always sketching, even when you were supposed to be doing other work."

"I know. I was a brat, wasn't I? I'll bet there were times you wanted to throttle me."

Michael smiled. "There were times."

"Art is an interest that never left me."

He kissed her hair. It was soft and silky against his lips. He wanted to kiss her again, but he didn't trust himself so he kept the conversation going. "Tell me about it. What do you paint with? Watercolors? Oils?"

She touched her lips to his throat branding him with a fire that instantly radiated through his body. "Mostly acrylics. I'm too impatient for oils and too impulsive for watercolors."

Michael tightened his arm around her. He wanted to kiss her so badly that it was hard to be patient. But by Laura's own admission, she was too impulsive, and that was what he was afraid of, that tonight was nothing more than an impulse for her, and that tomorrow she would have regrets.

"The next time we come here," he said, "it'll be in the daytime. This place is totally different but just as beautiful by daylight."

"I'd like that," she said. "I'll bring my paints."

Chapter Thirteen

Laura woke to the upbeat chatter of her clock radio. She opened her eyes and noticed the early-morning light filtering through her curtains. It was going to be another beautiful day. She hugged her pillow and snuggled under the blanket.

Last night was a dream. It had to be. Michael had been gentle and tender. And the way he kissed her— he loved her. He loved her! Wow!

It was hard to believe that yesterday she had awakened with no hope, and today . . . today she was going to meet Michael for lunch.

She jumped out of bed and hummed her way to the bathroom. A quick shower and then she would fix breakfast for her father.

She was still humming as she flipped the breakfast pancakes.

Her father came into the kitchen. "What's all this music so early in the morning?" he asked.

"I'm just feeling good."

He gave her a knowing grin. "It seems to me, you came home pretty late last night, young lady."

Laura smiled and poured her father a cup of coffee. "I guess it was a little late," she said. She put the cream and sugar on the table. "Here you go, Dad." She handed him a teaspoon. "We're having pancakes this morning."

"Is this a special morning?" he said. "I'm afraid to ask what we're celebrating."

"We're not celebrating anything." She got the butter and the maple syrup and put them on the table. "I just felt like making a nice breakfast, that's all."

Her father smiled. "It's nice to see you happy, Laura. It's been a while since I heard you singing."

"It's such a beautiful day that it makes me feel like singing."

Her father's smile widened. "I'm not going to ask any questions."

Laura blushed. "It's such a nice morning that I think it's a good omen for Mom, too," Laura said. "Do you think she might eat a pancake if I brought it in to her?"

"No sense waking her up. You know she doesn't eat much breakfast these days. You may as well let her sleep. She'll have a tough enough day coming up."

Laura loaded a stack of pancakes on a plate and set it in front of her father. "Here you go, Dad."

"Thanks." Her father put a big pat of butter on the pancakes and reached for the maple syrup.

Laura put two pancakes on her own plate. "You're right. I'll let Mom sleep. She doesn't need to wake up for another hour. I'll wait and fix her some toast and a soft-boiled egg before we go." She poured herself a cup of coffee, and sat down with her father. "What are your plans for the day, Dad?"

"I'm going to start the south field. Bobby said he'd come give me a hand trucking the grain." He scooped a big fork full of pancakes and maple syrup into his mouth.

"I saw Mr. Sweeny the other day. He said something about you and Mom going to Arizona for the winter, and Bobby tells me you and Mom are thinking of moving into town. What are your plans?"

"Bobby's folks are the ones going to Arizona, not us. We've thought about moving to town. We can be closer to the hospital and everything," he said. "The farm's getting too much for me, even now that the livestock's gone. I'm getting older. Maybe it's time."

"Why not, Dad? Sell the farm and buy a house in town. You and Mom can live comfortably. There's no need to work yourself to death on this farm."

"I don't want it to go to strangers. I've put too much of myself into it. Your mother loves this place. You kids grew up here. It's got lots of memories."

"He may be your only son, but you can't expect Ron to give up his career and come home, Dad. He never wanted to farm."

"No, I don't expect your brother to come back, nor your sister—not with that city husband of hers. I've given up on them a long time ago," he said. "But you . . ."

"Not me either, Dad," she said.

Her father didn't seem concerned. "You never know," he said.

Later, when Laura brought her mother a breakfast tray of soft-boiled egg, toast, and orange juice, she was pleased to find her mother looking chipper.

"This is a nice treat, dear, but you shouldn't have bothered. I could have gotten up."

"You're going to have a long day, Mom. I just wanted to give you a good start."

Mrs. Hart took a small sip of orange juice and set the glass down. "I've had these tests before," she said. "They're not very pleasant, but they're not as bad as you think. Don't worry, dear. I'll be fine."

Laura hoped so. She wanted, more than anything, for her mother to be fine. She didn't know what the tests consisted of, but her father had told her that they were arduous, and her mother tired easily. She knew that by the end of the day, her mother would be exhausted.

"Have some toast, Mom."

"I don't think so, dear."

"Come on, Mom, just a little." Laura cut a sliver of toast and dipped it into the soft-boiled egg. "Taste this. Tell me if I did it right."

Mrs. smiled. "You boiled the egg just fine," she said, and she took a mouthful and then one more.

Laura hovered over her as her mother took few more sips of orange juice and ate a little bit more of the toast and egg.

On the drive into town, Laura chattered about this and that, trying to keep the conversation upbeat. The last thing her mother needed at this point was to worry.

"You were late coming in last night," her mother said. "It seems to me that Shep was barking off and on for half the night."

"I'm sorry if I woke you."

"No, don't feel bad. I was awake anyway. I had a little trouble sleeping."

Laura looked at her mother's pale thin face with the deep dark shadows under the eyes. "Was it pain, Mom?"

Her mother shook her head. "No, it wasn't the pain. I guess I was a little nervous about today. It's nothing to worry about. I always get nervous when I have to go in for tests. But tell me about your evening? How was it?"

"Really good, Mom. I had a good time." She thought of Michael holding her and kissing her, and she got goose bumps.

"You're shivering," her mother said. "I hope you didn't catch cold last night."

"No, I'm fine."

"Well, what did you and Bobby do? Tell me all about it, or is it too private?" Her mother gave her a mischievous smile.

"We went to the school and played volleyball. There were about a dozen of us."

"Who else was there? Do I know any of them?"

"You know. Susan and Mary and Frank and Jake and Don . . . And then the group went out for pizza afterwards."

"So that's where you went."

"I didn't go."

"Oh . . ." Her mother was thoughtful. "Well, what did you and Bobby do, then?"

"Nothing."

"You did nothing for an awfully long time," Mrs. Hart teased.

At least she wasn't too sick to tease, Laura thought, but she said, "Mom, I'm not a child. I've been dating for quite a few years. I can take care of myself."

"Maybe so, but next time bring him into the living room."

Laura looked over at her mother. She wondered what her mother would think if she found out that it wasn't Bobby who had kept Laura out half the night. She decided to keep the information to herself.

"I didn't want to wake you, Mom."

"Thank you, dear. You are a good daughter. I couldn't ask for better, but don't worry about waking me. Next time, bring Bobby in. Keep safe from temptation."

Laura noted that in spite of the lecture, her mother was happy that Laura and Bobby had something going.

When they got into town, Laura helped her mother into the clinic, discussed with the nurse how long her mother's tests would take, and waited with her mother until she was settled in a bed.

"I'll be fine, Laura. You can go now," her mother said.

"I can stay a while longer."

"There's no need to stay. The tests are going to take all day," her mother said.

"I know. The nurse told me you won't be ready to leave until after four o'clock."

"Don't worry about me. I'll get some rest between tests."

"Okay, I'll go downtown and see what's in the stores."

"Buy yourself something nice," her mother said.

"Is there anything you would like me to buy for you, Mom?"

Her mother shook her head. "No, I don't need anything," she said. "Now go and have a good time, and I'll see you at four."

"Okay, Mom. Good luck on those tests. I'll be back before four o'clock." Laura kissed her mom's cheek and left.

She was going to meet Michael for lunch. She checked her watch. She had a two hours and fourteen minutes before she was to see him.

Her last year's fall wardrobe was still in fashion, and since nobody in Providence had seen it, it could be considered new. She really didn't need any new clothes—well, maybe one smashing outfit that would knock Michael's socks off.

Laura browsed in all the familiar boutiques, trying on dress after dress. With each one, she wondered what Michael would think. The final choice came down to two dresses: a black curve-fitting dress with a crossover "V" neckline that would certainly catch his attention, and a creamy white angora sweater dress that begged to be touched. Neither was subtle.

"I'll take them both," she told the salesgirl.

She continued to comb the stores. And then, in the window of the Wool Shop, she saw the most perfect, soft cuddly sweater in her mother's favorite shade of green—hope-green. She went in. The sweater was a small size, but so was her mother. She had gotten so thin and frail that it would fit and be just the thing to keep her warm as she relaxed in front of the television set or sat up in bed reading a book.

Laura bought it. Of all the purchases, this was the best.

It was getting close to noon. She had time for one more quick stop at the bookstore before driving to the restaurant where she was going to meet Michael.

She got into her car, and on her way across town, she drove past the park. She recognized what looked to be his van parked on the street. It was his van. She pulled into a parking space and looked around for Michael.

She saw him in the park, sitting on a bench, but he wasn't alone.

Laura felt a sick pain when she realized that the person with him was Sheila, the girl he had been with in the restaurant the other night. Laura felt guilty spying on him, but she couldn't help herself. As she watched Michael and Sheila, she saw them talking and smiling. The scene looked so natural. Then, Michael leaned over and kissed Sheila.

With a queasy stomach and blurry eyes, Laura put her car into reverse and backed it out of the parking space. Then she drove to the bookstore and wandered up and down the aisles, looking at the books. Their titles had no meaning. All she saw was Michael and Sheila.

There was no way she could have lunch with him now. There was no way she could face him, no way she could eat.

She went into the next store and then the next one. There was no pleasure in looking when she had so much trouble seeing.

She was to have met him at noon. High noon, she had called it. Wasn't that when people got shot down. Well, Michael, she silently told him, I guess you won.

Chapter Fourteen

Michael was worried about Sheila's reaction to what he was going to say. He had to break it off with her, and it had to be face to face. When he phoned her to arrange their meeting, she had suggested the park.

As he sat on the park bench waiting for her to arrive, he thought to himself that this was a good place for what had to be said. It was just public enough to discourage dramatic scenes and private enough to be able to speak freely.

Sheila arrived right on schedule, gave him a quick embrace, and then sat down beside him.

"I need to talk to you," he started.

But Sheila didn't give Michael the chance to break it off. She took the initiative. "I need to talk to you, too, Michael," she said. "I don't know quite how to say this. It's just that our goals are too different."

"Our goals are too different," he agreed, wondering where this was leading.

She was fidgeting with her hands. That was the only indication that she was nervous. "I don't want to hurt you, Michael," she continued. "It's not that I don't care for you. If you would just move to a city . . . it wouldn't even matter which one . . ."

Michael couldn't believe it. Sheila was making it easy for him. "I'm happy in Providence, Sheila. I have a role. I make a difference. Maybe it's because we moved around so much when I was a kid," he said. "I never really got to feel like I belonged anywhere. In Providence, I belong. There's something about living in a small town . . . It's what I want."

"Well, I guess that's it, then. You won't live in the city and I could never live out there in the sticks." She looked a little sad, but definitely not heartbroken. Michael was relieved.

"I'm sorry," he said, "and I appreciate your candor."

"I'm sorry too, but it's just too much of a sacrifice," she added. "You can't ask that of me."

"No, I can't, and I won't ask you to make that kind of sacrifice," he said. "We had some good times together and I'm going to miss you, but you're right, we're too different. You need the excitement of city life."

Sheila made one more attempt. "Are you sure you won't change your mind, Michael?"

"I can't change what I am," he said, "not even for you. You are a beautiful and charming woman, Sheila. You'll find some lucky man who will make you happy. It just can't be me."

She nodded. "Well then, I guess that's all we have to say to each other, isn't it?"

"We can wish each other luck and a good life."

"Good luck, Michael, and have a good life," she said. She looked sad as she added, "I am going to miss you."

She was a pleasant and attractive woman. They had shared some pleasant times. He would miss her too. "Good luck to you too, Sheila. Take care of yourself," he said, and he leaned over and gave her a kiss.

They parted friends.

Michael left the park feeling lighthearted and happy. He was going to meet Laura for lunch. He would sit across from her, watch the sun glinting in that mane of fiery hair, touch her hand, and maybe after lunch they would drive off to some secluded spot and they would kiss like they did last night.

Now, as he waited in the restaurant for Laura to arrive, he was completely happy. He had never imagined that Laura might love him. Last night had come as a blessing.

He ordered coffee, took a little notebook and pen out of his breast pocket, and turned to the page with today's list of errands. He had managed to do them all. Good—that meant his afternoon was completely at Laura's disposal.

When half an hour passed, he began to be concerned. An hour went by, and now Michael was getting quite worried. What could have happened to Laura? He tried to be calm, to banish visions of Laura injured or in distress by telling himself that she might have just plain forgotten to meet him—trading one pain for another.

By one-thirty, he was frantic. He would telephone

her home. If anything had happened, her father would be the first to get the message. He dialed the number and her father answered.

"Mr. Hart, this is Michael Foster," he said. "I'm looking for Laura."

"Laura's not at home," her father said.

Michael didn't want to worry her father, but he had to find out. "Do you know where she might be?"

"She's gone to town," her father told him. "Took her mother in this morning."

He knew that. But where was she now? "I'm sorry to trouble you, but it's rather urgent that I get a hold of her. Do you know when she's coming home?"

"She and the mother will be home by supper time." After a moment Mr. Hart added, "Do you want to leave a message for her? I'll give her your telephone number, if you want."

"Thank you very much, sir, but that's all right. I can call back later."

Next, Michael telephoned the hospital.

"Yes, Mrs. Hart is here," the receptionist told him. "She will be released later this afternoon."

"Do you know who is picking her up?"

"Her daughter will be taking her home."

"Is Miss Hart there now?" he asked. He could feel a knot of dread. Had something happened to Laura? Michael waited while the receptionist checked.

"No, Miss Hart hasn't arrived yet. She should be here around four o'clock. Do you wish to leave a message for her?"

"No, thank you. I'll catch up with her later." He tried to calm his fears. She must have forgotten to meet him for lunch.

It was almost two-thirty, and still no Laura.

He decided to go to the hospital. If she was all right, she would come to pick up her mother, and he would see her and find out why she hadn't shown up. There had to be a logical explanation.

He got in the van and sped to the hospital.

"Mrs. Hart?" the nurse asked. "I'm afraid you're too late. Mrs. Hart has already left."

"Already left? It's only three-thirty. When I called, you said four o'clock."

"Her tests were finished early so there was no need to keep her here any longer."

"Do you know who came to get her? Was it her daughter?"

"Yes it was."

"Was she all right?"

"She was fine, as far as I could tell," the lady said. "Why are you asking? Is there a problem?"

"No, there's no problem," Michael said, and he sighed with relief that Laura was all right. But unfortunately, she didn't love him.

Laura drove in silence while her mother slept.

The shopping bags in the back seat were a reminder of how happy she had been earlier in the day. How could Michael have been so false? Last night she was positive that he loved her, but he was obviously stringing her along.

And how awful for Sheila, too.

What a sleaze. The way he had held her and kissed her and pretended he loved her. That was pretty good pretending.

Laura felt a sick feeling in the pit of her stomach. No, he never did say, "I love you." He never said the words. She had been the one who talked about love.

What a fool she had been. She could feel herself blush with humiliation.

"What's the matter, Laura?" her mother said.

Laura looked at her mother on the seat beside her. "Nothing. Why do you ask?"

"You looked so strange, angry. And you were talking to yourself. Did something happen?"

"It was nothing. A car cut too close in front of me, that's all," Laura said. "It's okay. You can go back to sleep."

Her father and Bobby were sitting in lawn chairs, relaxing. She parked the car and her father immediately came to the car.

He opened the door for his wife. "How did it go?" he asked her as he helped her out of the car.

"Not too bad. We finished early." She let him help her into the house.

"You look pretty tired. Are you feeling okay?" Laura saw the tender way her father looked his wife and the way she looked back at him. He was so gentle with her mother, so concerned about her, that just seeing them together gave Laura a lump in her throat. Would she ever find that kind of rightness with a man?

Last night she had thought she had. Last night Michael had made her feel wonderful, loving, loved.

"How's your mom?" Laura was startled by the sound of Bobby's voice just beside her.

"Hi, Bobby. She's pretty tired," she told him. She opened the door to the back seat and took out a couple of packages.

"Here, let me help you," Bobby said. She handed them to him and reached for the remaining bags. "Looks like you did some heavy-duty shopping."

"Yeah, I guess I did get carried away." She headed

for the house, went into her room, and dropped the bags on her bed.

Bobby followed her into her bedroom. "I'm making progress," he said, handing her the packages. "Next thing you know . . ." he indicated the bed.

"Don't hold your breath!" she said. "Out!" She knew Bobby was teasing, but she wasn't in the mood to be teased.

Bobby threw his hands up in surrender and backed out of her room. "I'm out."

She shooed him into the kitchen. "I'd better get supper started," she said. She switched on the oven, opened the refrigerator and found the lasagna casserole she had prepared in advance, and put it in to bake.

Her father came into the kitchen. "Your mother's exhausted," he said. "I just put her to bed."

"Well, Laura, did the doctors tell you anything?"

"Not much. They said they won't have any results until Wednesday or Thursday. It's the long weekend," Laura said.

"I guess all we can do is wait."

Laura prepared the salad. Bobby wasn't saying much.

"I just about forgot," her father said, "There was a fellow called you on the telephone this afternoon."

She knew who called. After all, she had stood him up. He was probably so arrogant that he couldn't imagine anyone standing him up. "I'm not expecting any calls," she said.

"He said it was urgent but he didn't leave a message. He said he'd call you back."

She didn't say anything. There wasn't anything to say.

Her father wouldn't let it go. "He said his name was Michael Farmer, or something like that."

"Foster. What did he want?" she asked, opening the refrigerator and looking inside.

What did he want with her now? All she'd ever been to him was just a little bit of small-town amusement. Laura felt her face redden with hurt and embarrassment. How could she have been so stupid to think that he loved her? How could she have loved someone who was so two-faced? She closed the refrigerator.

"I don't know. He didn't say. Like I told you, he said he'd call back later. He seemed quite anxious to talk to you," her father pursued.

She shrugged. "He can call back all he likes. I'm not interested in anything he has to say. Supper will be ready in about half an hour." She sat down with Bobby and her father.

The telephone rang.

Laura didn't move to answer it.

It rang again and again. On the fourth ring, Mr. Hart said, "Do you mind getting that, Bobby?"

"Hello," Bobby answered the phone. "Yeah, she's here." He held the receiver out to Laura. "It's the coach."

"I don't want to talk to him. Tell him I'm busy . . ."

Bobby gave her a strange look, but then he spoke into the mouthpiece. "She can't talk to you now, coach. She says she's busy." He listened a while. "I'll tell her you called."

He hung up the telephone and turned to Laura. "I've never seen you behaving like this, Laura. Why do you have to be so rude to the coach all the time? As far as I can see, he treats you decent. What's wrong with you?"

Laura could feel the irritation rising. Why couldn't they just leave her alone. "There's nothing wrong."

"Did the coach say something to upset you?" Bobby persisted. "I'll bet you two had another fight when he brought you home last night."

Laura's father sat up in his chair. "Wasn't it you that brought her home?"

"No, I went for pizza with the gang."

"What about Laura?" Mr. Hart asked.

"Laura didn't want to come with us. She said she needed to get home early, so Mr. Foster was the one that brought her home." Bobby turned back to Laura. "So what happened, Laura? You were in a weird mood last night. Did you aggravate him into saying something to you?"

"No, I did not. Why is it always my fault? Maybe it's his fault? You men are all alike. I hate you all!"

"What are you saying, it's his fault?"

"Nothing. Just stop it, Bobby, okay."

"What did he say to you this time? Did he put you down?"

"No."

"I don't care what, he's got no right to nag at you and put you down. I'm not going to stand for it." Bobby was getting angry. He was back in his old role of protector, and Laura knew that once Bobby got the notion that she needed looking after, it was pretty tough to talk him out of it.

Laura exploded. "He didn't do anything, and I don't need anybody to fight my fights for me any more. Just leave me alone, Bobby. Please leave me alone." She burst into tears, ran into her bedroom, and closed the door.

Chapter Fifteen

Michael filled a box with his favorite paperback books, stacked it on top of the other book boxes, and began filling the next one when there was a loud knock at his door. He went answer it, but by the time he got to the door, there was another knock, even louder and more insistent.

It was Bobby Berent and he looked upset.

Michael opened the door wide. "Hi, Bobby. Come on in." He had always liked Bobby. There was nothing artificial or superficial about the boy. He wasn't brilliant, but he was good-hearted, and whatever he was feeling was right out there for all to see. Tonight was no exception.

"What's the problem?" Michael asked.

"I don't know, coach. Maybe you can tell me."

"What do you mean?" Michael asked. It had to do with Laura, he was sure of it. But what? Did Bobby know about last night?

"You and I have got to talk," Bobby said.

Michael nodded. "Maybe we do," he said. He should have expected this. He'd seen the way Bobby looked at Laura, and there was no doubt in his mind that whatever was coming, it had to do with Laura. "Want a Coke?"

"No," said Bobby.

"All right then, what's eating you?"

"It's Laura," Bobby said.

Michael was silent, waiting for the explanation.

Bobby went on, "I've never seen her like this before."

"Is it her mother? Is she worse?"

"Her mother? No, it's got nothing to do with her mother," Bobby said. "It's you."

"Me?"

"I don't know what happened when you drove her home, coach, but Laura's real upset with you."

What was Bobby trying to tell him? That Laura was upset because he had kissed her? She had been a wonderful loving woman last night. What had happened to change her? Why didn't she want to see him? Michael couldn't make any sense of it.

"You say she's upset. What do you mean? How do you know that she's upset?"

"How do I know?" Bobby barked a laugh. "When Laura's upset, you can't help but know it."

Michael could certainly agree with that. But it still didn't make sense. "Did she say anything to you? Did she say what she's upset about?"

Bobby shook his head. "She says she doesn't want to talk about it. That's what she says."

Michael paced back and forth across the room trying to understand. Did she think he had taken advantage of her?

"What did you say to her, coach?"

Michael shook his head.

"You must have said something," Bobby insisted.

What did he say to her? In a way, maybe he had taken advantage of her. He should have dropped her off at home, not tried to seduce her in the moonlight. But he hadn't seduced her. "I've got to talk to her," he told Bobby.

"Oh no, you don't. Laura doesn't want to talk to you. I don't think she even wants to look at you," Bobby said. "And, I'm sorry to say, coach, that means you've got to stay away from her."

"I can't stay away from her," Michael said. "Not unless she tells me to herself. I'm sorry, Bobby, but I have to talk to her. I have to find out what happened, why she doesn't want to see me."

Bobby's hands became fists. "I don't think you understand. Laura's my girl, and she doesn't want to have anything to do with you. I think you're going to have to find yourself another teacher to take her place, because I'm not going to have her coming to school and getting upset."

"I don't believe she sent you here to tell me that she's not going to teach," Michael said. "She's a grown woman, Bobby. She's going to have to do her own quitting."

Bobby's hands balled up into fists again as he took a step toward Michael. "Maybe I didn't make it plain enough. I've always liked you, coach, but Laura's going to be my wife and you had better leave her alone."

Michael felt a sick sinking feeling in the pit of his

stomach. "She's going to be your wife? Are you saying she agreed to marry you?"

"That's right. And nobody's going to make her unhappy, not if I can help it."

Well, that was that. "Okay, Bobby, I'll leave her alone." Michael said. It would have been hard enough to take the news before last night, but now, the thought of Laura with somebody else was almost unbearable.

Bobby suddenly smiled. "I'm glad we got that straight. I like you, coach. I didn't want to have to fight you."

"Fight?" Michael shook his head. "No, there's nothing to be gained by fighting. Congratulations, you're a lucky man."

Bobby beamed. "Thanks. I guess I am lucky, at that, but I'm surprised to hear you say it. I thought you'd give condolences. You never did like Laura much."

"That's not true," Michael said, but Bobby wasn't listening.

"Not that I blame you, the way she used to smart-mouth you. But you don't really know her," Bobby went on. "If you did, you'd like her. Oh yeah, she's got a temper, but she's really sweet and good-hearted, and she's a lot of fun to be around." He walked over to the couch and sat down. "I'll take that Coke now, if the offer's still open."

Michael went to the refrigerator and got two sodas. He handed one can to Bobby and snapped open the other.

Bobby waved his can at the half-empty bookcase. "Looks like you're moving."

"Yeah."

"Are you moving into one of those new apartments they just put up over by the arena?"

"No," Michael said. "I bought myself a place a few miles out of town. I'll be living out there."

"You bought yourself a place?" Bobby looked impressed. "You mean you're going to stay here in Providence permanently? Are you going to farm?"

"Yes, I do plan to live here permanently, but no, I don't have the time or the know-how to be a farmer, at least not for the time being," Michael explained. "The place I bought is just pasture land and some trees. I plan to get a couple of horses, some livestock . . ."

Bobby finished his Coke and crushed the can with his hand. "That went down good," he said. "Got another one?"

"In the fridge," Michael replied.

Bobby got himself another Coke. "How was basketball camp?"

"It went all right. We could have used your help."

"I missed doing it but I was just too busy this year." He took a big gulp. "My dad's gearing up for retirement, so he's letting me run the place. That, and Laura's dad needed help this summer, what with Laura's mom being so sick and all."

"Maybe next year," Michael said. So Bobby was helping Laura's dad. Not even married yet and he was already part of the family. How could he hope to cut into that?

"Maybe," Bobby agreed. "By the way, how's this year's team looking?"

"Pretty good."

"Have you got some good players coming up?"

"It should be a strong team again this year." Michael's mind was not on the conversation. All he could think about was that Laura was going to marry Bobby.

Bobby was a good guy—good company. The only thing wrong with him was that he had Laura. No, not yet. Michael had to talk to her one more time, had to be sure it was true before he would give her up. He'd told Bobby he'd leave her alone, but . . .

"Are you still going to coach now that you're principal?"

"Yeah, I have trouble giving it up. I guess I enjoy it too much. There is a young phys. ed. teacher who's keen to coach. We'll try teaming it. See how it works out."

"I could maybe come and help out sometimes," Bobby offered.

"You could," Michael replied. "So, you're marrying Laura," he added. "I guess I shouldn't be surprised. You two were going out in high school."

"We've been going out for as long as I can remember," Bobby said. "There was never any other girl for me."

"And how about her? Were you the only guy for her?"

Bobby grinned. "I guess."

When Bobby left, Michael went back to his packing. He wanted to get everything boxed and ready to move. Tomorrow would be a big day, his first day in his new home.

Michael had bought the old Martin property in late spring and had worked on it all summer, trying to make it liveable.

The place had been a disaster of rubbish and garbage, but not any more. He had installed a trailer hitch on his van, purchased a utility trailer, and carted off load after load of cans, boxes, rusty tools, broken crockery, and old boots to the garbage dump. After that, he had gotten to work on the improvements.

The old log cabin had only two rooms and no indoor plumbing, but it was quaint and it was solid. The first improvements were a well and a septic tank. Then he added a section at the back of the cabin for a small bathroom, a utility room, and an office.

After that, Michael had stripped and cleaned and scrubbed the interior, put in a new wood floor, modernized the small kitchen, and added electricity and a telephone. It was spartan but cozy. Originally, he had thought of it as the ideal cabin—great for fishing or hunting or just getting away—but after all the work he had put into it, the cabin became more and more appealing as a place to call home. So much so, that he had given notice on his furnished apartment over the Providence Barber Shop, gradually moving his belongings into the cabin. Just a few more boxes and he would be completely moved in. His own place. It had a good sound to it.

Michael stood in the doorway and looked around. The place looked good. The old pot-bellied stove that Mr. Martin had used to heat the cabin had been polished and shone as the centerpiece. Michael had added electric heating, but he looked forward to sitting by the cozy old stove when winter came.

Someday he might build a real house on the property. It would be a great place to raise a family. A barn, a few horses, a garden, pets for the kids. The only problem with the picture was the hole where Laura should be. The only woman he wanted in his life was unavailable.

He walked down to the river. In the daytime it was even more beautiful. If Laura could only see it now.

He should never have brought her here the other night. He imagined her by the river, under a tree, in his house. She haunted him.

But Bobby had said she didn't want to have anything more to do with him.

But that night was something he'd never forget. Oh, how he'd wanted her, and for a while there, she had wanted him too. It must have been the moonlight that had bewitched her.

Thank goodness he hadn't lost control. He had been right to wait until daylight before he asked her to make up her mind, before she made a commitment.

Chapter Sixteen

Laura heard her father's footsteps on the porch indicating that he had finished his morning chores and was coming in for breakfast. She turned off the stove, put the hash brown potatoes and the scrambled eggs into serving bowls, and set them on the table. She filled his coffee mug and then she disappeared into her room. This was one Saturday morning she didn't feel like facing anyone.

"Laura," Mr. Hart called. "Laura, come on out here and have some breakfast."

"I'm not hungry this morning," she said through the door.

"Well, come on out anyway. It's time we had a talk."

She knew that tone of voice. She'd have to face him sooner or later, so she may as well get it over with.

She took a deep breath, squared her shoulders, and

put a smile on her face. She came into the kitchen, got herself a cup of coffee, and sat down at the table.

Her father was eating his breakfast, but when she joined him, he put his fork down and studied her. "You want to tell me what in blazes is going on around here?" he asked. Even though he spoke roughly, she could hear her father's concern, and it made her feel like crying.

She forced herself to smile. "Nothing's going on, Dad. What makes you think there's something wrong?"

"Something is going on," her father said. "You're acting strange, and Bobby's mad as heck at this principal of yours. What I want to know is, does Bobby have any right to be mad?"

She looked him in the eye. "Bobby doesn't have any rights with me, Dad. I've told him that, and I've been trying to tell Mom, and trying to tell you, but none of you seem to listen. None of you seem to care what I think."

Her father was thoughtful. He picked up his fork, took a mouthful, chewed it, and swallowed before responding, "And this other man, does he have any rights?"

Laura held her breath. How did her father know? Had she been that obvious? "What other man?" she asked. "What do you mean?"

"Are you in love with the school principal, girl? Is he the reason you don't want Bobby?"

A lump formed in her throat. She took a sip of her coffee. "How I feel doesn't matter. He's not in love with me."

"You were out with him the night before last, and

it seems to me you were out pretty late." Her father's voice had become gentle.

Laura didn't reply. A blush suffused her face as she remembered the feel of Michael's arms around her. At the time, it had seemed so right.

"And then yesterday morning, if I recall correctly, you were like a meadowlark—all sunshine and hope." Her father put his fork down. "Bobby seemed to think the problem happened when this Foster brought you home, but as I see it, whatever happened, happened yesterday. Do you want to talk about it?"

"There's nothing to say, Dad," she said. When he silently waited for her to continue, she added, "He's got another girl."

"You're sure?"

"I saw him with her."

"And because of that, you're going to give up? That's not my Laura." Mr. Hart shook his head. "The girl I used to know went after what she wanted."

"I can't go after him, Dad. I've wanted him for a long time, and all that time I was sure I never stood a chance with him. And I could live with that." The lump in her throat hurt unbearably, and suddenly the tears started to flow. "But the other night, I thought that maybe he felt something too. I was wrong. He was just playing me for a fool."

"You're talking about the man that was phoning all day yesterday?" her father asked. "It seems to me, you're the one who's being the fool."

She wiped her eyes with the back of her hand. "What do you think I should do?"

"You're making accusations and you're not giving him a chance to answer them." Her father pointed a finger at her. "You can talk to him, hear his side of it. That's the least you can do."

"He was kissing her in the park," she exploded. "How can he explain that away?"

"It don't hurt to let him try."

Laura was silent. Maybe her father was right. Maybe she should let Michael explain. She vacillated between wanting to believe her father and feeling anger at Michael's betrayal. It was betrayal. She wasn't blind and she knew what she saw.

"Bobby says you're going to give up teaching. Is that true."

"Of course not. Why would I quit my job? You know me better than that."

"Well, I'm glad of that," he said. He got up from the table, took a plate out of the cupboard, heaped a spoonful of eggs and a spoonful of hash browns on it, and put it in front of her. "Here, you'd better have something to eat," he said.

After her father left for the fields, Laura threw herself into her work. The only way to take her mind off Michael was to be too busy to think about him.

She stripped the sheets off the beds, collected the towels and dishtowels, gathered up all the dirty clothes, and took everything downstairs to the laundry room, where she sorted it into several piles on the floor: sheets, towels, whites, delicates, work clothes. She filled the washing machine with sheets, put in the soap, and set it to start.

Then she hurried upstairs, took the vacuum cleaner out of the broom closet, and thoroughly suctioned the dirt out of the living room carpet.

Her mother was lying on the couch, crocheting. "What are you doing, Laura?" she asked.

Laura passed the dust cloth over the windowsills. "I'm just getting the place cleaned up, Mom."

"You're just like a whirlwind," her mother said. "The house can't be that dirty."

"It's not bad, Mom. I just thought I'd best get it done while I have the time."

She finished dusting and asked, "Where do you keep the furniture polish?"

"I think there's some in the cupboard near the washing machine," her mother said.

Laura ran downstairs, found the furniture oil and a clean cloth, and proceeded to polish the old oak dining room table and chairs.

Mrs. Hart stopped working on her afghan and watched Laura. "Something's got you in a knot, Laura. Do you want to tell me what's the matter?"

"It's nothing at all, Mom."

"Is it me you're worried about? If it is, stop worrying. I feel much better today."

"You're looking better, too. I'm not worried, I just have so much to do." She heard the *ping* that signaled the washing machine had gone through its cycles. "Time for the next load."

She hurried downstairs, put the clean clothes into the dryer and loaded the washing machine with delicates, mainly lingerie and blouses. Then back upstairs to vacuum the bedrooms.

By noon the laundry was done and folded, the entire house was vacuumed and dusted, the furniture was polished and the mirrors were cleaned.

Laura prepared tomato soup and tuna sandwiches and called her father to come in for lunch.

"What can I get you, Mom?"

Mrs. Hart put the kettle on for tea. "I'll eat with you and your dad. Those sandwiches look wonderful."

Laura's heart felt like bursting. This was the first time her mother had indicated an interest in food in quite a while. Maybe she was getting better.

After lunch, Laura got back to doing some schoolwork.

She took out the binder of Michael's notes. She felt angry enough to throw them in his face, but that would be a stupid thing to do. She might as well get some use out of them.

The telephone rang. It was Mary and her voice was bubbling with excitement.

"Hey, Mary. You sound pretty happy. What's up?"

Mary was full of chatter. "Wasn't it great playing volleyball the other night. All the old gang . . ."

"It was a good time," Laura agreed.

When the exuberant Mary hung up, Laura got back to her schoolwork. Michael's books, Michael's writing, Michael . . .

Maybe she had been wrong to refuse to speak to him. After all, she was the one who stood him up. He had every right to be upset with her. She wanted to call him and apologize for having missed lunch. It would be the polite thing to do. But what about the scene in the park? What about the other woman?

He doesn't love me.

But what about Thursday night—the way he had kissed her? The way he had held her? Was that nothing more than a bit of moon magic?

Her father said she should give him a chance to tell his side of the story. Maybe he was right.

She walked into the kitchen, flipped through the

telephone book, and dialed his number. Then she held her breath as she waited for him to answer.

One ring, two, three, four, five rings. There was no answer. He wasn't home. She hung up the telephone and paced impatiently around the kitchen. She dialed again and again there was no answer. She went in to check on her mother. Mrs. Hart was asleep.

Laura had to get out, had to clear her head. She took a sheet of paper and wrote: Mom, I've gone out for the afternoon. Supper is in the oven in case I'm late coming home.

She took her paints, her easel, and a canvas, got into her car, and kicked up a cloud of dust on her way out the gate.

The Martin place—she would go and paint the Martin place.

Chapter Seventeen

It was mid-afternoon when Michael telephoned Laura's house. After four rings, Mrs. Hart answered the telephone and she didn't seem too thrilled to hear his name.

"No, Laura isn't at home," she said.

"Do you know where I can reach her?"

"No, I don't know where Laura went. She doesn't need to ask my permission any more," she said. "Maybe she's gone to school. She seems to go there a lot."

Michael thanked Mrs. Hart and asked her if she would please give Laura the message that he called. Then, he got in his van and drove to school. Her car wasn't there. He doubted that she was there, but he went to check just in case she was in her classroom. She wasn't there.

She must be at home, refusing to talk to him, he thought. It wouldn't be the first time that her mother covered for her. He wondered what Laura had told her parents about him. Had she misunderstood his motives? And had she told her parents and Billy that he had tried to seduce her? Was that why they were all conspiring to keep him from seeing her? She couldn't have. Why would she have?

He got back in his van and drove out to the Hart farm.

When he turned into the driveway, he was greeted by loud barking as the dog came out to investigate his arrival.

"I suppose you're telling me to get lost too," he said. He reached out and patted the old dog. The dog rubbed up against him, asking for more. Michael laughed and scratched him behind the ear. "If only Laura was as easy to deal with as you are."

Laura's car wasn't in this yard either. Her mother must have told the truth. He knocked anyway. He may as well talk to her mother, face the music.

"You're the principal," Mrs. Hart said. "Laura's not here."

"Mrs. Hart, may I talk to you? I won't take up too much of your time."

She stood looking at him, obviously trying to decide whether she should listen to him or not.

"Please," he said. "It's important."

She opened the door. "Okay, come in."

"Thank you." Michael entered.

She led him into the living room and indicated one of the armchairs. "Sit down. Would you like a cup of coffee?"

"No coffee, thank you. I know you're not well, so I'll just stay a few minutes," he said. He sat down and waited until she had gotten comfortable on the couch before broaching the subject. "I came to talk to you about Laura."

Mrs. Hart gave him a chilly look. "I remember a telephone conversation a few years ago. You wanted to talk to me about Laura back then. What's the problem this time?"

Michael sighed. Obviously, Laura's mother liked him even less that Laura did. Maybe this hadn't been such a great idea. "The problem is me," he told her.

She looked surprised. "You? That's a surprise."

"I'm in love with your daughter." The words just slipped out. They were not the ones he had meant to say, but when he heard them, he knew they were right.

Mrs. Hart studied him for a long time, and then she smiled at him. Her smile turned into an amused little laugh and Michael noticed the mischief in her eyes. He waited for her to speak.

"So you are the problem," she said, still smiling, and Michael sensed that Mrs. Hart was no longer the enemy. "What do you want from me, young man?"

"Bobby told me that she's going to marry him. If that's what she wants, well that's it, but I need to hear it from her."

"Don't you believe Bobby?"

"I don't know if it's true or not," he said. "I love her and I have a feeling that she loves me too, but for some reason—I'm not sure why or how—things have gone wrong. I have to talk to her but I can't get near her. She won't even take my calls."

"If you know Laura, young man, you realize that she makes up her own mind about things," Mrs. Hart said. "I can't make her see you if she doesn't want to."

"I know, but would you let her know I was here. Please ask her to call me."

"Can you tell me why I should? I don't know anything about you other than you made her miserable. I know Bobby is a good man who's willing to take good care of her. The way I see it, she'll be a lot happier if you stay out of her life."

She sounded harsh, but her eyes seemed more amused than hostile. Michael had the distinct feeling that Laura's mother was enjoying the exchange.

"You can't live her life for her, you know. She has to be the one to decide."

Michael got up from his chair. "I'd better go. Thanks for listening, and believe me, I'm not the ogre you make me out to be."

"Maybe not. Good luck, young man." Mrs. Hart started to get out of her chair.

"Don't bother getting up. I'll see myself out," Michael said. "And, thank you."

Where to now? He may as well move the rest of his belongings over to his new home. He headed his van back to his apartment to pick up another load.

Michael's van was loaded down with boxes of books, a duffel bag of hockey gear, another bag with his tennis racket and assorted sports equipment, his computer and printer, a desk lamp, a table lamp, a potted cactus, and a stack of clothes still on hangers. He drove carefully, mindful that his load could shift.

When Michael eased his van into the driveway, he spotted Laura's car parked at the far end of the yard, down by the river. Had she come looking for him?

It was too good to be true. His first reaction was to rush right to her. This was his chance. He'd better not blow it.

Afraid he might scare her off, Michael parked by the gate and walked up the lane to where he found her standing behind her easel, engrossed in her art.

It wasn't him she had come for. She had come to paint. She much for another chance to win her. But still, she was here.

She had her back to him as she concentrated on the intricate details of the landscape she was painting. He didn't want to break her mood so he stood in the background, shaded by the trees, and watched as she added bark to a tree trunk, highlights to a bush, texture to the path.

The picture on her easel looked almost finished. He wondered how long she had been there. It must have been a while.

She had painted the river, the trees, the clearing, the fire pit and the hollowed out riverbank where they had sat side by side and shared their feelings. All that was missing was them.

He watched in silence as she continued to add final touches: a little more color to the clump of trees across the stream, some highlights on the ripples in the river, a few reflections in the water. He noted that even though it was a beautiful day with the bright sun shining and the vibrant colors of the landscape glowing, Laura's painting was melancholy.

Michael wanted to approach her, to put his arms around her, but instead, he kept his distance, willing her to turn and yet afraid that when she saw him she would leave.

Laura stood back and looked at her painting. Then she added a touch of blue to the shadows.

Two nights ago, the scene had been all silvery and

magical. She had been in a fairy tale, and Michael had been her prince.

She closed her eyes and remembered the feel of his lips on hers.

Why had he not taken advantage of the moment?

She forced herself to stop thinking about what could have been. Instead, she concentrated on the scene in front of her. Michael had told her that this place was beautiful by daylight, and he had been right. It was a beautiful, romantic place.

Romantic . . . because he had been here?

She had noticed the old cabin among the trees when she had driven into the yard. Someday she would come back and paint it—maybe later in autumn when everything was golden, or maybe in winter. In winter it would be beautiful. She imagined the cabin, it's lines softened by the naked trees and cuddled by a soft eiderdown of snow. It would make a striking painting.

She dropped the paintbrush into the little jar of cleaner and turned. It was then that she saw him, standing motionless in the middle of the path. She felt her heart drop to her stomach, leaving her chest empty and hurting. She had wanted to talk to him on the telephone, not face to face. Face to face was too difficult.

"Hi, Laura," he said. He didn't move.

Her heart was back in her chest and pounding so that she could hardly hear herself think. "Hello, Michael."

"I've been looking for you."

She swallowed and nodded. What was it she had wanted to tell him? She couldn't think, she couldn't breathe. It was like being frozen in time, just like her painting.

"Please don't leave," he said.

Leave? How could she leave? Why would she leave?

He took a step toward her, moving slowly, with his hand outstretched. He looked like someone reaching to stroke a rabbit or a deer. "I'm sorry if I did anything to hurt you." His voice was gentle, soothing.

Her mouth was dry and her voice came out croaky. "What do you want, Michael?"

"I want to talk to you about the other night," he said, still moving toward her. "I want to apologize to you."

He wanted to apologize, but that wasn't what she wanted from him. She wanted him to explain, to tell her he loved her, to tell her that she had made a mistake, that it had been someone else in the park, not him. She didn't want him to apologize. She stared at him speechless.

"I shouldn't have brought you here," he said.

Oh yes, you should have, she thought.

"It wasn't fair to you," he said.

Why not fair? Because of gorgeous Sheila? She turned away and began to pack up her paints. She didn't want him to see how much she hurt, and she certainly didn't want to hear about how he was in love with someone else.

"Well then, why did you bring me here?"

He didn't answer her question. Instead, he said, "I should never have kissed you."

So he was admitting that kissing her had been a mistake, that he didn't care about her. He was just feeling guilty about having been disloyal to his little Sheila. What was he looking for? Sympathy? Absolution? Why not? Suddenly she felt better. Michael had hurt her, but she would never let him know.

"Why should you be sorry over a few kisses?" she said. She tossed her head and looked him in the eye. "We didn't do anything wrong, and anyway, I haven't given it another thought."

He looked disappointed. "You mean that the kisses didn't mean anything to you?"

She continued to stare him down. "Not really. No more than they meant to you."

Michael was silent for a moment. "So why did you come back here if the other night meant nothing to you?"

Laura shrugged. "To paint, of course. You told me that this place was beautiful by daylight. You were absolutely right." It was getting easier and easier to play the charade. "I was thinking that someday, I might come back and paint that cabin."

Even though Laura's voice was calm and she acted casual, Michael could sense the tension that was gripping her.

He had wanted to tell her that he loved her, wanted to ask her if she loved him, but somehow, once again, they had gotten sidetracked. Every time he tried to get near her, they ended in an argument and it was happening again. How on earth was he going to get her to let down her defenses long enough to listen to him?

He tried to keep the conversation positive and impersonal. "You like the cabin?" he asked.

"It's perfect in this setting. It gives a feeling of continuity—a solid reminder of the past."

"Do you want to have a closer look at it?" he asked.

She nodded in agreement. "It's time I pack up my paints."

"Can I help you carry anything?"

"Sure." She pointed to the painting on the easel. "But be careful with it, it's wet."

She picked up her paint supplies, and led the way to her car. Michael followed with the painting. When it was all put away in the trunk of her car, he led the way to the cabin and she followed him.

She peered in through the window. "It's really nice in there." She sounded surprised.

Michael opened the door. "Come on inside."

She seemed hesitant. "We can't do this, Michael. This is somebody's home."

"It's my home," he said. He wanted her to see it, to approve of it. "Please come in."

Her eyes widened. "Yours?"

He wondered if it was with disbelief or amazement. "Yes. I thought you knew," he said.

She shook her head. "You never said."

"I came out here fishing with Mr. Walsh a few times and I fell in love with the place," he said. "When it came on the market, I couldn't resist."

"I heard it was a real mess."

"It was. I've worked all summer getting it fit to live in. Come on in and have a look."

She stepped through the door ahead of him. "Oh, Michael, this is great," she said. "I love it, especially that old stove."

"I like that old stove too. It was here all along. I just finished cleaning it. Everything else, I brought. Come on, I'll give you the grand tour." He led her to the kitchen corner. "This is the kitchen. It's pretty small, but it's functional."

"It's a wonderful little kitchen. Everything looks so new."

"It is. I imagine Mr. Martin used the old stove for cooking as well as heating, and there used to be an old table in that corner," he said. "The first thing I did, after cleaning the place up was to put in electricity, running water, and plumbing. The cupboards and the appliances have only been here a couple of weeks."

"Do you live here now? I thought you lived in town."

"I'm just about moved in. All I need to do is bring the rest of belongings over here." He opened the refrigerator. "Would you like a glass of wine?"

Laura hesitated.

"You're my first guest."

"All right. A glass of wine would be nice."

"Feel free to look around while I open the bottle. All there was to this place was two rooms, this large one and a smaller one that I'm using for my bedroom. I wanted a bathroom and an office so I built an addition on the back."

"Okay." She was all bubbly enthusiasm again.

Michael found a bottle of white wine and two glasses. He took out a box of crackers. "Do you like smoked oysters?" he called out. "Or would you prefer cheese with your crackers?"

"Either one," she called back from the back of the house. "But don't go to too much trouble."

"No trouble at all," he said. He opened the oysters and stuck toothpicks into a few of them. Then, he put the open can on a plate and placed crackers around it. Not bad, he thought.

Laura came back to the kitchen. "This is a wonderful place, Michael. I love it."

He handed her a glass of wine.

She held her glass up and toasted. "To your new home."

They drank to that and then he held up his glass, "To you. May you be a regular at this table." He noticed that Laura looked flustered, so he quickly offered her a cracker.

"Where would you like to sit?" he asked. "On the sofa or in a straight back chair."

"I'd rather sit in a chair."

He grinned and she rose to the bait. "It's not because I'm afraid to sit on the sofa with you."

"Well," he said. "If you're not afraid, then I'd just as soon sit on the sofa. It's a little more comfortable." She looked uncertain but then she went and sat down primly on the edge of the sofa.

Michael sprawled beside her. He watched her fidget and take an inordinate interest in studying each of the objects in the room. "Do I make you nervous?" he asked.

She blushed. "Of course not."

Michael felt a surge of hope. He did affect her. No matter how hard she tried to conceal it, he was sure that he did affect her. But there was Bobby . . .

"Bobby came to see me last night. He said that you plan to quit teaching." Michael watched for her reaction.

Laura looked surprised. "Quit teaching? Why on earth would I do that?" She looked at Michael. "He said that?"

Michael nodded.

"What else did Bobby say?"

"He said you two are getting married and I'm supposed to stay away from you. Is it true?"

"No, no, no, no! I don't know where Bobby gets these notions," she said and then added, "Actually I do know. It's Mom and Dad and Bobby who have my life all planned out. It makes me so angry. Don't I get any say in what happens to me?"

Michael was ecstatic. She wasn't going to marry Bobby.

"Of course you get the say. It's your life," he said. He reached out and touched her hair.

She leaned toward him.

"Laura," he said. "I have to tell you something."

She stiffened. "You don't have to tell me anything."

He reached for her hand and she pulled it away. "Please listen," he said.

She jumped up and headed for the door. "No!" She sounded as though she was going to cry.

He stood up too. "Wait, Laura," Michael shouted at her back. "I love you!"

She stopped and turned, and the look she gave him was totally unreadable. He waited for her to say something.

"I love you," he repeated. "This is not the most romantic way to tell you, but you need to know."

He held out his hand to her and she gave him hers.

"I want you to be my wife," he said.

And then she came into his arms. "Marry me," he whispered. "Please marry me."

Tears blurred her eyes. "Oh, Michael, I've loved you for so long," she said. "Of course I'll marry you. Yes, yes, yes." She threw her arms around his neck and kissed him.

"But you have to know that I still have commitments. I have to help out at home."

"Sweetheart, I know that. We'll work something out," he said. "Now come here." His lips came down on hers and she knew that everything would turn out just fine.